Getting to Paris

First edition, March 2018
Copyright © 2018 Stephanie Gidley

Published by Penciled In
5319 Barrenda Avenue
Atascadero, CA 93422
penciledin.com

ISBN: 1-939502-27-6
ISBN-13:   978-1-939502-27-8

Cover illustration by Madison King
Book and Cover Design by Ben Lawless

Text is set in Garvis Pro, Fira Sans and Argenta

Getting to Paris

By Stephanie Gidley

Contents

Paris — The Dream. 1

Learning The Language —
First Class, Private Lessons, Duolingo . . 9

Hosting a Foreign Exchange Student —
A Failed Language Experiment. 17

Learning the Language —
Another Try, Conversational Class. 24

Reading in French. 32

Coffee Break French. 38

Saving Up Money 43

Foreign Exchange Online. 58

Inviting a Friend 69

A Travel Companion For Myself. 77

Travel Tips From Madame Seidler 83

Creating My First Itinerary. 93

Working with Travel Agents. 99

Planning with Marybeth: Two Heads Are Better
Than One, Or So You Would Think . . . 107

Planning with Aunt Mary 119

French Language CD's
From the Library. 136

Conversational French Class,
the Second Time 143

Private Lessons with Aunt Mary 153

Building Anticipation 164

Getting to Paris — Literally
(Car, Planes, and a Taxi) 176

Adventures on the Trip: Paris 190

The City of Beaune 216

Last Stop, the French Riviera
and Nice. 235

Reflections After the Trip. 252

About the author. 263

Dedicated to my family:
to my husband Jeff,
and to my children Michael, Carissa,
and especially to Rebecca who was my first editor.

Getting to Paris

Chapter 1

Paris – The Dream

For as long as I can remember, I have always been interested in Paris and all things French — French people, French cities, and French culture. Also, how they live, how they speak, what they eat, how they dress, how they raise their children, and more. For years I've read books, magazines, and articles online about all of these things. I knew I wanted to one day visit France, and Paris especially, but how does a regular, middle class, American suburban wife, mom and teacher *get* to Paris? Especially when her husband has no interest in going with her? How do you plan for it, save money for it, and actually make it happen?

I believe this interest in all things French was instilled in me by my parents. While I was growing up, my mother and father both talked with pride about our family being originally from France. My mother never studied her genealogy but knew enough about her family tree to know that her family originally came from France before settling in the French area of New Orleans. My father on the other hand has studied his family history extensively and followed it up to the point of his family's arrival in the United States from France, but never got a chance to follow the lead into France itself. Even though studying the genealogy wasn't my interest, the French culture in general, was.

My mother was also quite a francophile. Francophile: A person obsessed with every-thing French, yes that describes her well. My mother often read interior and design books about French homes and always had a magazine in the house with beautiful photos of the French living spaces. My mother also read many books on the French diet and embraced the same healthy eating habits of the French in our home, although she admittedly did not cook the same way. She researched a lot about French fashion as well. Not the fashion of the models on the runway, but the classy and chic looks of the everyday wear of the Parisian women. She raised us to dress well every day with makeup and hair done when going out. There were no sweatpants or the ultra-casual look in our home that is so popular now.

Since I grew up being exposed to so much about the French culture, naturally I grew to be a Francophile as well. I tried the French diet as I struggled to eat healthy as a teen, I took French language classes in high school, and I even got interested in the home decor. One home interiors look my mother was always fond of was the "French country" look and in the early 80's that look was popular in the United States as well. When I was a teenager, I bought myself a light blue comforter, and a small wicker basket filled with silk yellow and white daisies, and redid my bedroom in the French blue and yellow look that was found in all the magazines.

As an adult, I looked to my mother's examples and the French culture as well. As a young wife, I carried the French country look into my own home and often flipped through my own French home decor books and magazines to find out more about it. I began to become interested in the French fashion principles too, giving up wanting to own many outfits and due to a tight budget as well, wanting instead to pare down as the French women do, to simple capsule wardrobes of several key, quality pieces instead.

Raising children was both a pleasure and a challenge. Again, I looked to the French for inspiration on this topic. For diet, I took tips from the book *French Children Don't Get Fat* by Marisa de Belloy, which pointed out to me all of the reasons why I should *not* fill my children with sweets and unnecessary snacks. For discipline, I found out that the high expectations that the French have toward their children's behavior coincided with mine. Their attitude on how children were to act at the dinner table, treat their siblings, and give respect to grown-ups were right in line with my thinking. I even found French articles online to go along with my teaching philosophies. As an elementary school teacher, I am often confronted with students that have been misdiagnosed with behavior disorders and I was pleased to read that in France those disorders are non-existent or very rare and children's poor behavior is handled with firm guidance by the parents and teachers instead, again confirming my philosophies of how I raised my own children. When I shared an online article about this with my family one time, they answered back, "of course mom, you *would* find something French to back you up on that, too."

As I grew older, it was the language that interested me the most. I was fascinated by this group of people that communicated in a completely different language, and I wanted to learn that language. I took French language classes in both high school and college. When starting to think about and plan this trip, I wondered how much I could remember now. I began to consider taking lessons again and I was eager to try speaking it once more.

Of all things French, the thing that fascinated me the most was *Paris*. I would read about it in books or see it on TV and in movies and it always seemed so romantic, mysterious, and interesting. Of course, I thought of it as the center of France, where the culture stemmed from and was the highest point of the French culture when it came to everything else; food, fashion, and people. I wanted to go there more than any place in the world.

Somewhere in my early-40's I decided that if I was ever going to get to Paris then I had to make a goal. I am a firm believer in setting goals and then working slowly towards them with many small steps until they are accomplished. I decided that I was going to go to Paris before I turned 50. I began talking about it, often telling family and friends about this goal, hoping to cement it in place and take ownership of it. I knew I would have to learn the language, save money, and make a plan. I had several years to do it and I got started right away.

Chapter 2

Learning The Language – First Class, Private Lessons, Duolingo

I began learning the French language in high school. I took four years of it there and then went on to take 3 more years of it in college. At the time I was planning to double-major in Elementary Education and French but time and money pushed that plan to the side when I left school early to get married and have my first child. I ended up finishing my degree in teaching about 15 years later when I went back to school after my youngest was in 1st grade, but by then my French was mostly forgotten.

I decided when I got my first teaching job that I was going to keep on going to school but this time I would go back for French lessons. Realizing that French classes at the university were not going to work for my schedule or budget, I happened upon a flyer at our corner grocery store. The teacher, Madame Seidler, was a local who was from Paris herself, and she taught classes out of a small church near where I lived. I emailed Madame Seidler with questions, asking which class I should take, beginner or intermediate? She assured me that with my high school and college classes, I was capable of coming to the intermediate class, so I signed up and attended the first class, eager to learn.

The class itself was wonderful, albeit, over my head. My eyes were wide open as

I sat there and listened and I realized that I had no idea what anyone in the class was saying. I took notes furiously, looked words up in my French/English dictionary, and basically just tried to keep up. At the end of class Madame Seidler assured me that this was the class for me and that I would catch up in no time. I attended several more classes and made friends in the class who helped me out. One such friend, Lorraine, even gave me a couple of French workbooks and a French verbs book that she had gotten at a library sale. The intermediate class was based a lot on vocabulary, textbook exercises of verb tenses, and discussions of textbook stories, so these books that Lorraine gave me came in handy. At the end of the school year, French class ended for the summer. Being a teacher myself, I had some spare time over the summer and I poured over the French workbooks intent on catching up by the next fall. I diligently did one lesson a day, reading and writing, and much of what I knew before came back to me.

Fall arrived and I was doing better, although not as well as my perfectionist personality wanted to do. Taking these classes helped me to be a better elementary teacher as well though. It opened my eyes to things my students might be experiencing when they learned new things or were struggling in class. One such incident I remember was when Madame asked me to read out loud. I read a whole paragraph, proud of my accent and getting most of the words correct. I was surprised, however, when she asked me to explain the content of what I had just read and I realized that I could not remember a single thing. It occurred to me that the same thing was happening to my students when I was working with them on reading comprehension. Not only did they need to work on their comprehension while reading, but I did as well!

The following semester, I thought it would be money better spent if I hired Madame Seidler for private lessons instead of the class. I thought it might be more personalized and that we might be able to talk more conversationally, which had been my original goal: to be able to talk with French people in their own language. As it turned out, the private lessons were a bit more academic than I expected, with focus mostly on vocabulary, textbook exercises, and talking about articles in books that didn't really have much to do with me or my regular life. I don't think I communicated very well with Madame and what I was hoping to get out of these lessons. I decided to focus on teaching myself.

I had heard about a free online course for language called Duolingo. Basically, you go on your computer, tablet, or smartphone and work through lessons and all the basics of a language in order to fill up a "tree" to make it golden, showing that you have learned the language well. I worked on it, but made slow progress due to my schedule and limited amount of time. The following summer I decided to devote time every day to my online lessons and I diligently completed 20-30 minutes a day. At the end of every "level" a trumpet would sound and the course would commend you for how far you had gotten. I was excited to finish my "language tree" and when I got close I took out my cell phone anxious to record what I thought would be a tremendous flourish of trumpets sounding the notice that I had completed the full French tree! What happened instead was such a disappointment! The tree just ended with a little symbol of an owl and the message, "you have completed your tree." No trumpets, no flourish, nothing special. I laughed and sent my video to my 25 year old daughter to share the disappointment. I knew she would appreciate the joke because I had told her all about Duolingo and she was trying it out for herself as well.

I figured at least I would have increased my knowledge quite a bit and after all, that was really the point. I went to another area of the language site and clicked on a progress test. The last time I had taken one I scored around 50% with a 2.85 out of 5.0. This time I thought for sure I would score close to 100%. Once more it was disappointment. I scored 1.77, what was I doing wrong? Again, I laughed at the absurdity of it and then I gave up on Duolingo for awhile.

Later, reflecting on my Duolingo, I determined that I must have remembered just enough of each lesson to complete each level but that I did not internalize the information enough to remember it. I decided that I would continue the online lessons periodically but now just as a refresher and that I needed to find another way to learn the language where I would really internalize it and remember it.

Chapter 3

Hosting a Foreign Exchange Student – A Failed Language Experiment

I had always been interested in hosting a foreign exchange student. When my first two children were younger my husband did not share the same interest and basically vetoed it every time the subject came up. A couple years after I decided I was going to go to Paris before I was 50, we got an email from our youngest daughter's high school asking for host families. It immediately caught my attention. My husband received the same email at his work email address and said that he just laughed to himself thinking, "Here we go!" I thought it would be a great opportunity! I could practice my French with her (of course we would host a girl) just as she would be practicing her English with me. Also, I thought we would be able to make a connection with her family so that when we went to France, we would have actual French people to talk to and not be just tourists.

We thought about it and talked as a family about it. By now our older two children had moved out on their own and we had only our 15 year old daughter still at home. She was going to be a sophomore in high school. This would be the perfect age and we had room in our house, so we all agreed that the timing seemed right and we called the exchange student leader to sign up.

Of course, we were only interested in a *French* foreign exchange student because of my French interests. Students from there are few and far between we were told so it was a good thing we were calling early, in the spring, to put in our request. Soon, we were matched with a 15 year old girl from France, Marie-Lou. We contacted her over the summer and got to know her by email and FaceTime. We finally met Marie-Lou the week before Labor Day, one week before school started when she arrived in our city.

We got Marie-Lou enrolled in school and encouraged her to join an activity. We explained that most teens in our school either participated in a sport, a club, had a job, or did all three. She chose Cross Country so we signed her up for the team and she started practicing with them right away. Our daughter introduced Marie-Lou to her group of friends, we got school supplies, and the school year began.

I was excited to begin talking to our student in French! One day I simply asked her in French "Pouvons-nous parler en francais?" *Can we talk in French?*

Marie-Lou answered with a smile "Oui, bien sur!" *Yes, of course!* And then it was silent... I didn't know what else to say.

I laughed and tried a few things like, "Le ciel est bleu," *The sky is blue,* or "Comment ca va aujourd'hui?" *How are you today?* Marie-Lou answered politely. I couldn't think of anything else to say so the conversation ended with a laugh from me. I tried speaking French with her on other days too, thinking ahead of time of a few things to say. Each time I engaged our student in conversation, it went the same way. Marie-Lou would smile and say, "Of course!" and answer any questions I asked, but then she would not add anything to the conversation. I began to feel funny about it.

Later, I heard Marie-Lou say in a conversation to someone else that she was here to speak English, not French. She wasn't talking specifically about my attempts at French with her, actually our friend had asked her if she missed speaking French while she was here. The comment Marie-Lou made to our friend suddenly struck me as so obvious though. Of course! What was I expecting? I laughed to myself. She was a 15 year old girl! What would any typical 15 year old girl do? They would answer, just as she did, but they wouldn't add much to the conversation. I was picturing her saying things like,

"Ok, what would you like to talk about? Let's talk all about your day." Or, "Let's talk all about your work," or "Let me explain to you all of the French words for everything in this room - such as window, counter, etc."

This is what a grown up would do, someone my age perhaps, but certainly not a 15 year old girl. How could I have been so wrong? I laughed to myself as this occurred to me and shook my head with a smile.

Over the course of the year, we did learn *some* French from Marie-Lou. Every day when I came home from work we asked each other, "How was your day?" I eventually asked her how to say that in French.

She told me, "Comment etait ta journee?" and I spoke it in French every so often when I asked her. Also, my husband got a kick out of asking her what some French words were and as she told him, he would use them around the house. Marie-Lou thought this was very funny! She taught him things like "Je ne sais pas" — *I don't know* — and "Je ne comprend pas" — *I don't understand* — and he used them all the time.

In the end, alas, our family never did

become close with Marie-Lou's family, mostly due to differences in how we both raised our teenage daughters. So, our experiment failed as to learning and practicing the language, *and* in getting to know a French family whom we could visit when we traveled to France. Oh well! C'est la vie!

Chapter 4

Learning the Language – Another Try, Conversational Class

Mid-way through the school year of hosting our student from France, when I realized I wasn't going to be able to practice my French with her as I expected, I signed up for a conversational French class. This was a step up from the intermediate class I took before but it was with the same professor, Madame Seidler. In the past, I had been very afraid to take this class. I thought you had to speak very well to join this class but Lorraine, my friend from the intermediate class told me that she attended the conversational class on occasion and that she didn't really speak as much as listened to others in the class and their conversation. I figured now was as good a time as any and I signed up.

Driving to my first class was nerve wracking. I didn't know what to expect. When I went in, the professor greeted me and introduced me to the others. They were all very nice but as soon as I opened my mouth I felt like I had forgotten any French I had learned. I sat in the class without saying much the whole time. I felt completely lost and hardly understood anything. I thought "here we go again." It was just like at the other class. I sat hunched over my notebook, doodling on the side. I was afraid the professor would ask me a question that I didn't know how to answer so I avoided looking at her. I left that night feeling terrible about the whole thing.

That week I was watching some TED talks online about teaching and I came across one by Amy Cuddy about body language and confidence. The speaker talked about studies they had done where people *sat* in powerful positions, as opposed to vulnerable positions and how it affected their attitude. She talked about hunching over notebooks, doodling, avoiding eye contact, arms crossed - all the things I had done in class! I realized my body language showed how I felt inside. The speaker went on to talk about "power positions." How some people in a study were told to sit up, look around, open their shoulders, and sit attentively and how that changed their whole attitude.

Next, Amy taught about how people prepare for presentations by going into a room beforehand and *standing* in "power positions", hands on hips, making muscles, arms outstretched, etc. while giving themselves pep talks, and how this helped them not only feel better, but perform better. I recognized myself in what she talked about and thought I should use this at my next French class.

During school the next week I taught about these methods to my third graders. I told them what had happened at my last French class, how I felt and how I responded to how I was feeling. They were inspired and very interested in the method I had learned from the TEDtalk and were willing to try it before their next test. We did all of the moves together for 2 minutes just as the speaker had recommended. Then the students took the test and they all said that they felt better about taking it after trying our new plan.

On my way to the next French class I tried the same methods on the drive there. I also went into the bathroom before class and did some of the moves in the stall to prepare my body as well. It seemed awkward and funny to me just as it had to my students, but I was willing to give it a try.

In class I sat in a "power position" with my head up, shoulders back, and made eye contact not only with the professor but also with the other members of the class. I didn't speak much but I definitely felt better and also seemed to even learn a bit. I left the class feeling much more confident about it than before.

I kept explaining to my students along the way about how challenging the French class was for me and how it was good for me to keep trying. I think this example of how I was struggling helped them to see how to work hard and persevere at something and to not give up. These are skills we teach daily and that students, and everyone, needs to continue to improve at.

At the next class I spoke two whole sentences! It doesn't sound like a lot but it was a lot to me. I answered a question from the professor *and* asked a question myself. Each week I improved just a little and I also understood the conversations a little bit more.

At the end of our spring term of ten classes, my professor planned a dinner party at the church where we took our classes and invited a real French chef to cook for us. The other members of the class had met this chef on previous occasions but this would be a first for me. I was excited and anxious. I wondered if we would speak in French during the whole dinner just as we did in class or if we would be allowed to speak in English at all.

At the dinner I was bound and determined to talk to the best speakers in our class and to find out how they had gotten so good at speaking the language. I had never taken the opportunity to discuss this with them before. After each class, I was just too exhausted from focusing so hard the whole time or I was too shy to talk to my classmates about it. For professional development at my school, we had read a book called *The Growth Mindset* by Carol Dweck and we were learning how to utilize this information with our students. One way we taught the students to improve was that when they saw someone who was better at something than them, instead of thinking, "I'll never be able to do that,"they were to think, "I will find out how they got to be so good at that." This was where I got my inspiration.

At the dinner I spoke to many classmates a little bit in French and in English as well. I asked them how they learned French outside of class, how they practiced, and how they had become so fluent. I got a wealth of information from them. One told me about Coffee Break French, which is a free online website, app, and podcast that broke down the French language into easy 20 minute lessons, that you could easily listen to on your "coffee break." Another told me about French language tapes called the Berlitz tapes, and she said she listened to them about 1,000 times. Others watched French movies, and television shows or read books translated into French. I took all of this to heart and vowed to study intensely during my off time over the next summer.

Chapter 5

____

Reading in French

One thing that I did learn from Marie-Lou, our foreign exchange student, was that reading in English was in part what helped her to speak her second language so well.. She said she had read several books translated into English and was most proud of reading *Pride and Prejudice* by Jane Austen. She often read English novels with lots of dialogue in them as a way to improve her speech as well. Also, several of my friends from class recommended reading in French as a way to improve my language skills, so I thought I would give it a try.

I had read about a certain book titled *Clochemerle* in one of my France magazines.

It was written in 1934 by Gabriel Chevallier. After World War I, in which the author served on the front lines, he was disgusted with war and politics. In order to find peace and quiet, he retreated on the weekends to the countryside. There he wrote the book as a tongue in cheek account of politics in France at that time. He wrote about the real city Vaux-en-Beaujolais, but called it by the pseudonym "Clochemerle" in his book. Chevallier used this fictional city as an example of how local politics played out in miniature what was happening on the big stage in France as a whole.

It was touted in the magazine article as a satirical read with some bawdy parts. The article went on to explain that Vaux-en-Beaujolais had adopted the title of the book as a sort of "nick name" for their town, and that its residents enjoyed a famous status from having been used as a model for the city in the book. I thought it was great that the residents of Vaux-en-Beaujolais never took offense from the book, rather they took it for what it was, a comical version of what happens in daily life in small village politics, and laughed along with the rest of the book reading population.

The magazine article described not only the book, but also the town. The residents had painted murals of scenes from the book on many of their town buildings in the city center. They had erected some replicas of edifices from the book, had a museum built with memorabilia from the book and the author, and even named some of the local wine after the book and one of the main characters. Included in the city center are "talking" benches where tourists can sit and listen to audio versions of the book played out in French on one side of the bench, and in English on the other side. I thought this would be great for us if we visited this town while we were in France because I could listen to the French versions, and my daughters, who don't speak much French, could listen to the English versions.

I went ahead and ordered both an English and a French translation of the book from Amazon.com. I waited eagerly for them to arrive in the mail. My plan was to read a page at a time, first in the French translation, then in the English. I thought reading the books in tandem would give me the best sense of what happened in the story. I also knew this would push me to figure out everything I could in French first, with an easy way for me to check my answers by then reading it in English.

In reality, the French translation of the book was very difficult for me. I think because it was written so long ago, it was like reading an encyclopedia in French. There were many old fashioned words or literary words that I would not have learned in my French studies. I tried reading it with my French/English dictionary, going back and forth between the novel and the French translation pages, but this proved to be too time consuming.

As it was, I went ahead and finished reading the English translation. It was funny and the bawdiness wasn't much more than something similar to Chaucer's *Canterbury Tales.* The novel is about a power hungry mayor who decides to purposely wreak havoc in his town in order to gain the notice of politicians in higher positions who could help advance the mayor's ambitions towards a higher position himself. He had built a public urinal, directly in the center of the village, knowing full well that the citizens of the town would fight and bicker over it, which would draw attention from outside their little city and gain them some publicity in the the news. Among the bickering about this new structure, there was intrigue of some naughty nature by some wayward married women and men and a bit by the local priest as well. All in all it was an entertaining read and inspired me to research traveling to this city further, even though it did not help me accomplish my goal of reading in French. Were I to try this again, I would choose a modern book with simple words that I would recognize better. I may even try reading a children's book.

Chapter 6

Coffee Break French

Coffee Break French is a podcast of short twenty minute lessons that my friends at French class told me about when I asked them about the varied ways they all learned the language outside of class. Since I first learned about this in the spring, it was good timing because I could use some of my spare time in the summer to listen to these podcasts while I was on break from school and teaching.

I began by searching for these podcasts online. It took a while but eventually I came upon the website and the free version. I then sat and listened to the first one, pen in hand while I took notes. I decided to start at the beginning even though I am not a beginner with the language. I figured I could use the first few lessons as review and then go up levels from there.

It was incredibly boring to sit in the kitchen listening to these first few lessons. Even taking notes seemed tedious. I felt antsy and like I needed to be doing something more productive. Always the multi-tasker, I decided to download the podcasts on my phone and listen to them while I took a walk each day. I decided to also take my dog for a walk at the same time and was very proud of myself for essentially doing three tasks at once.

I began to become obsessed with Coffee Break French and focused on listening to not one, but two podcasts per walk. When I returned home each time, I listened to them again online while I did small chores around the house like washing dishes, folding towels, etc. I took notes while I listened and worked, hoping to reinforce the lessons for myself. I also thought I could then take my notebook wherever I went and read over my notes as another way of studying.

These lessons really helped me improve my grasp on the French language. Not only did I learn grammar and pronunciation, but I also improved my listening skills which was very important to me. I am a visual learner so I could picture French words well and often determine their meaning by the spelling, however I had a difficult time picking out words when I listened to French. These Coffee Break French lessons, helped me to really focus on listening while I walked and I could easily focus and pay attention to all of the nuances and important inflections in the language.

There are forty lessons per season of Coffee Break French, by the end of the summer I had listened to all of season one and two and was well on my way into season three. The lessons did get progressively more challenging but that was good for me and kept me moving forward. My notebook was small enough that I could drop it in my purse when I went out so I did that often and when I found myself in line waiting for something, or at an appointment waiting, I took out my notebook and studied rather than flip through magazines or scrolling through messages on my phone.

Sadly, when school began again I found myself with limited time to study once more. After working all day with 29 little ones, I didn't have the energy or the interest in going for a walk or studying with Coffee Break French. I tried listening at work on my lunch break but couldn't focus enough knowing all of the teaching tasks I needed to accomplish during that time as well. I kept my notebook handy but put off listening to more podcasts until school breaks such as Thanksgiving, Christmas, Mid-Winter break, and Spring Break. All in all, it is a great program and I would highly recommend it to anyone looking to improve their skills.

Chapter 7

Saving Up Money

In the fall of 2014 I turned 47. That is when it started to sink in that if I was going to really make my goal of getting to Paris by the time I was 50, then I had better start saving up my money. We are a typical, middle class family. We have a nice life but we don't usually have enough extra money for extravagant things such as traveling, so I decided to make a plan. I would start saving now, about $100 a month and then next year, perhaps raise it up to about $200 a month. In the meantime, I would also do my best not to spend any money on unnecessary extras and I would try to put aside that extra money as well.

And so I began. Each month I began to

transfer $100 out of my checking and into my savings account. I kept track on a little piece of paper that I kept in the back of my wallet since we had other money that went into that account as well, and we had some bills that were paid automatically from that account. I knew that saving would be a challenge and I didn't want to take the chance of any of my trip to France money getting mixed up with the balance of other money that was there.

I had done this before when I wanted to save up money for something that usually wasn't in the budget. My children and I used to take a ski trip once a year with friends, and money for that got put aside from the grocery budget or whatever I could skim from at the time, and I literally placed it in an envelope under my mattress. I did this as well when I was obsessed with buying a tandem bike for our cabin up north. My husband thought I was crazy, for wanting it and for the cost, so again, I saved up money little by little in an envelope under the mattress until one summer I had enough and I went and purchased a beautiful red tandem bicycle from the local bike store. I often tell my children, if you want something, you have to work for it little by little until you accomplish it, from saving money to baby steps toward a goal, you have to keep moving forward until you get what you were working towards.

Saving money, bit by bit, worked well for the first year. I had over a thousand dollars saved up but I knew I would need more. I started saving $200 a month. That year, after Christmas I assessed the situation again and knew I would not have enough saved at this rate and that I would need to start skimming money from other parts of our budget, meaning clothing and extras that I spent on that weren't all that necessary. My husband started to tease me saying that I was quite the tightwad and things that my paycheck went for in the past, such as extra dinners out, or small gifts here and there, were nearly non-existent during this time. I never kept cash in my wallet anymore because when I did, I was tempted to spend it. Whenever my husband checked to see if I had cash to cover something, I could honestly laugh and say I didn't have any. Jeff was totally on to me though and figured out that I purposely didn't carry cash anymore.

By 2016, I decided that I wasn't going to spend money on any new clothes for my wardrobe. For the spring, I told myself that I would just wear everything from the previous year to work, that I didn't need anything new, and besides, since I am a teacher, I didn't need anything new for summer because we mainly spent those days at home or up north at our cabin. For dressier times or for going out, I would keep the same philosophy, wear what I wore last year. If it was good enough for then, it would be good enough for now.

That plan worked well for the spring and summer but when fall arrived, I *really* wanted to go shopping. As a teacher, the fall always feels like a new beginning. When I was growing up, we didn't get many new things in our family of 5 kids, but one thing we did get was some new clothes each fall for school. I started back to school shopping for myself but then thought of Paris and had to ask myself, "What do I want more? Clothes or Paris?" Of course the answer was Paris so I needed to buckle down, come up with some stronger will power and another plan.

What better way to plan for France, than to dress as the French do? French women don't own a lot of clothes. They have what is called a "capsule wardrobe" that usually consists of about 10 key pieces that they mix and match along with accessories and they create their daily outfits from that. Personally, I have never owned a lot of clothes. Hearing others complain over the years about having too many clothes to fit in their closets, I started thinking about what that meant and teaching my daughters the concept by saying often "if you have too many clothes for your closet, than you have too many clothes."

No one can honestly wear all the clothes that typical American women keep in their closets. Many women keep clothes from when they were a smaller size, thinking that they will eventually get back to that size, so they hang on to them. Others keep clothes from many years ago when they were in style but aren't now. I have been guilty of that myself. I began going through my closet and dresser and getting rid of anything that didn't fit, or was out of style and paring my clothes choices down to items I really liked and would actually still wear. I was getting ready to plan my own capsule wardrobe.

I began researching online to see if I had some of the key pieces I would need. I had most of the basics, black pants, gray sweater, white blouse, a few pullover sweaters, etc. I actually had more than I thought once I had cleared out the clutter.

Not being that creative myself, there were only so many outfits that I could come up with after I saw what was left. Again, I went online for ideas. I found a couple blogs by women my age and I began to visit them each day. Cindy Spivey was one. I would take ideas from what she was wearing, and then look in my closet and try to put together similar looks. I also had access to some trendy pieces of clothing thanks to my teen-age daughter, but that is a fine line, find-ing something cute in her closet and then making sure it didn't make me look like I was trying to dress too young. *That* was not my intention at all. I was almost 50 and proud of it, not almost 50 and wishing I was perpetually 29.

Even with what I had saved and what I was saving monthly, I wasn't sure if I would have enough for my trip. I kept putting off thinking about it, believing that it would all work out somehow and that as the trip neared I would be able to gauge more of what my finances were and what the trip would entail and I would deal with the true cost of everything at that time.

My husband must have been having the same thoughts because on my 49th birthday he gave me a 50th birthday card with a large check in it and the sweetest note ever about this money going towards my trip. I was so surprised at the check that I didn't even realize he had given me a "50th" birthday card instead of a 49th birthday one. He asked "Do you get it?"

"No..." I had to admit. He explained that most people spend money on a big birthday party when they turn 50 and he knew that I was taking this trip instead of having a party so he thought it would be better if I got the money now and put it in my trip account instead of getting it when I turned 50 as a gift or to go towards a party. How thoughtful of him! He wanted me to be able to finish saving and planning and not worrying about the final cost of the trip and to enjoy the process. I started crying and I'm not usually emotional about gifts and such (Stress is about the only thing that makes me cry!). How sweet and indeed, now I could enjoy the planning process that much more.

Saving had to continue though, even with the influx of this check into my trip account. Christmas was coming up and as usual, I had a budget for it so I began shopping with my budget in mind. Just as with any Christmas however, once you start shopping, you start to see things that are out of your budget for those people on your list, or you start to think, "I just want to buy them *one* more thing." I struggled to stay on budget but I kept out of stores as much as possible and did much of my shopping online. We don't watch much tv in our house so I didn't see the loads of commercials and other ads promoting the shopping habit at this time of year. I focused on *doing* things with and for others for Christmas, and not *buying* things for them. When I did think of extra people to go on my list, such as volunteers in my classroom and such, I bought very small but thoughtful gifts for them, instead of over the top gifts like I may have been tempted to buy in the past.

Along with Christmas gift shopping, came Christmas outfit shopping. Again, we didn't spend much on clothes when I was a kid but we did get new clothes for fall and also a new outfit for Christmas so it seemed like the usual thing to buy. There would also be pictures of the family parties and I couldn't be seen in pictures wearing the same thing as last year, even if I did love the dress I had. I began to brainstorm and think of what I had that I could change up and make appear different. For the casual family party, I wore a simple black long sleeve dress with black leather on the shoulders, tights and boots and my bright red scarf, tied of course like the Parisians do. For Christmas Eve mass and the dressy family party, I wore a sleeveless black dress that I wore to a wedding with bare legs and heels in the fall, and instead, topped it this time with a bright red shrug, opaque tights and black heeled booties. Both of these outfits looked completely new to others and I wouldn't have come up with them if I hadn't been working hard not to spend money on new clothes at this time. I was proud of myself.

I got through the Christmas season, and indeed all of the whole clothes shopping seasons with my travel budget intact and my savings account right on track for paying for the trip in the spring. It hadn't been easy, but I found that you could certainly save a lot when you are purposeful about your money instead of spending on a whim.

Just a couple weeks before the trip, I got a sweet text from my oldest daughter, Rebecca. She has been working to save money herself for her own trip. I had really been on her a couple years before about starting to save money for our trip. She knew I couldn't afford to pay for her part as well but she was having a hard time getting started with saving. She kept putting off opening a savings account, and since she was making enormous payments each month on her college debt, she didn't have a lot of extra money to be saving for a trip, similar to my situation.

I sent her a small amount of money, $50, online one day with a note telling her to use this money to open her savings account for her trip with. I hoped it would be the motivation she needed to take that first step. It worked. She made time in her busy day to get to the bank and open her account and deposited the money I sent her. After that, about every other month, I sent her an additional $50. At first it was to remind her to be saving herself and to be putting money aside. Even though she had opened the account, she admitted that she still wasn't putting any or very little money into it. After a couple times of getting the money from me, she began to make a plan herself. She began by having some money taken automatically out of her paycheck to go into this account. Then she added more to it when she could. Rebecca is not much of a shopper, just like me, so she began adding money to her account that she could have used on shopping and that began building up her savings as well. Since she was diligently saving at this point, I continued to send her money just to keep her motivated and to help add to her total.

In the end, she had just what she had estimated for her trip and that's when she texted me. "THANK YOU, thank you for all of the times you sent me money to help me save enough, it really helped motivate me to save as much as I could too!" It is really nice to get a message like that from one of your children. It makes you feel, as a parent, that they really did take to heart a lesson that you tried to teach them, and that is really what it is all about.

Chapter 8

———

Foreign Exchange Online

I determined that I needed more practice speaking French out loud. I began researching online for some options. Meanwhile, one day while I was at Barnes and Noble bookstore, I was browsing through a book about French and came upon a section that explained about foreign language exchange websites where you meet people online who speak the language you are learning, and speak with them in exchange for them learning English from you. Not a bad idea, I thought. I would look into it.

While I was off work for a few days for Thanksgiving break, I thought I would begin by Google searching "foreign language exchange." Boy was I surprised to see several sites listed! I clicked on each one and tried to weigh the benefits of each therein and choose the one best suited for me. I ended up trying mylanguageexchange. com. I'm not sure what drove me to choose this one over the rest. I think it was because this one had suggestions for you to meet up and facetime with people, then gave a list of questions to answer together in each language, and encouraged you to use this list in order to "break the ice" with others and find common ground to talk about, without getting too personal.

This site had a profile section for you to fill out, a little like a dating site I surmised, but I reasoned that people on this site really were looking for a language partner and not a date, so I gave it a shot. I carefully planned out what I would say in my comments "American woman looking for French speaking partner." No, it shows that I'm American in the profile. "Happily married woman..." I thought that would fend off any would-be suitors. "Happily married woman, mother of three children, elementary teacher, seeking French speaking partner." Better, but not quite good enough.

I opted to read other profiles to get some ideas. Novel idea, of course that would be better than coming up with it on my own! Everyone else was much more casual, "Hi everyone! I'm here to meet people of the world and make friends!" or, "Hello! I am looking to meet others and practice another language, contact me." Some gave details about themselves which I thought was helpful in making a good match. Not having any experience with dating sites, I didn't know what I was really getting myself into. In the end, my profile stated, "Hello! I have been learning the French language for many

years but still consider myself only intermediate. I want to learn to speak better and
would love to learn while helping another
learn the English language. I am 49 years
old, and I am a teacher. I teach 8 year old
children in third grade. I am happily married and have 3 children. My son is 27 and
I have one daughter who is 25, and another daughter who is 16." My family often ac-
cuses me of giving too much information,
so I thought this was concise but still got
across a little bit about myself and my level
of knowledge of the French language. Then
I clicked around the site looking for others
that I might want to connect with. I found
a couple other women who seemed similar
to my age and sent them a message within
the site to make initial contact. On this site
you have two options, one, you can send a
"Hi!", for free and that lets the person know
that you are interested (again, seems similar

to a dating site), or you can send an email to them, but that requires a membership. I wasn't ready to commit to a membership yet so I just sent a "Hi!" to each of them. I logged out and waited to make contact with a few new friends.

After a couple days, I hadn't gotten any messages from the women I had contacted or any other would be "friends" yet so I went back online to look over my profile. I realized that I hadn't included a photo and thought to myself, "I wouldn't want to contact someone else if *they* didn't have a photo either." So I enlisted the help of my daughters in choosing a picture to upload. A few days later, I checked again and although I didn't get an answer from those women, I did have a few requests from others. At first I was so enthusiastic that I responded to all three that I got that day.

One was from a 27 year old, Simbo from

Paris. I thought 27 sounded young, and I mentioned it to my 25 year old daughter. "I don't really want to talk to a 27 year old, but I guess that is better than someone my age who might want to date me. Why do you think he contacted me?"

"Maybe he's thinking the same thing, mom" she answered. "Maybe he just wants to practice his English and not have to worry about talking to someone who wants to date him either." Good point! So I answered him with a short message.

Another was from a man, 57 years old. I had a similar thought about him but answered him nevertheless. He responded back wanting to make further contact rather than simple messages on the site, which means that he gave me his email address and asked me to contact him there. Something just did not feel right about it. When I went back to the site to view his profile, I noticed that not only was he 62, NOT 57 like his email stated, and his job title was listed differently, but that he didn't have a photo on his profile either. I simply responded one last time that I wondered why his email message did not match his profile and why he did not have a photo shown, and explained that I did not feel comfortable making further contact with him. My husband laughed when I told him all of this and said I could have just ignored his message. I said I wanted him to know why I didn't want to be his "friend" and my husband laughed again. "Your mother thinks she is going to fix the dating website world" he told my daughters.

Lastly, there was a message from Sylvie, a mother of 2 older boys, around my age. She sounded interesting so I messaged her back. She then gave me her email address and sent me a bit of a longer message about why she was learning English, her likes/dislikes, hobbies, etc. It took me a few weeks to answer her back because Thanksgiving break was over and I was back to work. In the meantime, it occurred to me that she did not have a photo included on her profile either. What is with these people? I thought. I finally sent her an email and explained that I didn't have much time for emailing while I was working full time (to write in French is hard and takes a lot of time), but that I was looking forward to getting to know her better and perhaps moving towards chatting online (which was my goal in the first place). I then inquired about her family and mentioned that I noticed that she didn't have a photo on her profile. I got a one line answer in return, "I am only interested in a regular pen friend", period. Well! Okay then! I wondered if her answer was prompted by my lack of speediness in reply and admitting that I didn't have time for regular exchanges, or from my questioning her lack of a picture showing her real self? Hmmm, sounded fishy to me.

In the following days and weeks, I got a number of varying messages. I got some messages from a few women, one who was Chinese but lived in France. She wanted to practice her English with me but I only wanted contact with *native* French speakers. One was French, but lived in America, and wanted to practice, but I wanted to converse with someone who lived in France. Then there were a few random others that didn't match my criteria either. They didn't have photos, or weren't French, or something else.

Most of the messages were from men. Some were young, some were old, some whose native language wasn't even French! One man was from Serbia, one from Germany, one from Turkey. Most of them stated that they wanted to practice their English for work...Most of those who contacted me, again, did not have photos! Those that did have photos, showed quite a variety. Some slim, some heavy, some sitting, some standing - one even had his shirt open with several buttons and several gold chains - all trying to look very debonair at the camera.

There was only ONE that I even remotely thought of answering, Nico from Nice. He was 52 years old, an engineer, and he didn't have to *try* and look debonair for the camera, he *was* debonair. Also, we were planning to visit Nice while we were in France! How fitting! I'm sure he was a very nice gentleman, he could meet us and show us around... right. My husband would *kill* me if I answered Nico, just as I would kill him if he made contact online with some beautiful woman. That was one thing my husband requested, jokingly about this trip.

"Do not fall in love with a Frenchman while you are there." Of course not! I begrudgingly deleted Nico's message, this time without giving all of the reasons why.

Later I got more strange messages from more men. I went back to the site and updated my profile to include, " I am interested in meeting married women, close to my age, who are looking to email and then chat in person online." There! I thought, that will put an end to those looking for a date rather than a language partner. Then came the worst message of all, from Alexandre, who did indeed include a photo on his profile. This one was of him lounging in a hot tub, steam all around him, hairy chest and looking very seriously at the camera. I burst out laughing. Nooooo! I deleted his message immediately and later that week, deleted my profile as well.

Chapter 9

Inviting a Friend

Originally, I planned to take this trip with my two daughters as my husband was not interested. He is a self-proclaimed creature of habit and I can hardly get him to go to dinner at a new restaurant, let alone go to a new country. It was a little bit sad for me that Jeff was not going with me but there was nothing to be done about that. My older daughter had traveled some in college and was interested in traveling more so she was in from the start. My younger daughter wanted to go too so I bargained with her that if she took French language classes in high school instead of Spanish, then I would include her in the trip.

My 25 year old daughter, Rebecca's plan was to go to France with us, then to England to visit her friend who lives there. She wouldn't be with us the whole time. In the meantime, her relationship with her boyfriend had gotten serious since we started planning this trip together, and she asked me if she could invite him. Of course that was fine with me. How could I say no to a young couple in love going to Paris together?

My 16 year old, Carissa, then began negotiating to bring along a friend as well. There was one friend that I certainly would consider saying yes to, her friend Janine, but I wasn't sure if her parents would allow her go with us or not. For one thing, *we* had saved up for a couple of years for this trip and they would have to pay for the whole thing in a few short months. For another thing, there had been a few terrorist attacks in France over the last couple of years, not to mention around the world, and I wasn't sure how another family would feel about the safety of this trip.

Besides that, I wasn't sure if I wanted this to be a trip just for me and Carissa to enjoy together, or if I was open to her bringing a friend. I knew in her 16 year old mind, a trip with her best friend would be so much more fun than a trip with her mother by herself, but I wasn't sure if I was ready to let go of the vision I had in my head of this mother-daughter bonding time. I told Carissa "no" to bide my time for a bit and thought about it and prayed about it.

I finally decided that I would ask Janine's mother privately. Then if she said no, Carissa wouldn't know the difference. So I texted Janine's mother one day, and told her about our plans, asking if there was any way that she would consider letting Janine go with us.

She texted back right away asking for more details. After we texted back and forth a few times, she said she would talk to her husband about it and get back to me. I was surprised but hopeful! Perhaps this would work out after all. I began to picture in my mind different ways of telling Carissa the news and was excited about seeing her reaction.

I waited a few days, tentatively, thinking that either way it worked out would be fine with me. I knew we would have a good time together by ourselves, *or* with her best friend, so I was fine with whatever the outcome would be. Finally, after work one day I got the text from Janine's mom that she and her husband thought it would be an exciting opportunity and that they would let Janine go with us. My heart skipped! I was so excited for Carissa! What 16 year old wouldn't be excited about taking a trip abroad with her best friend?

Janine happened to be over at our house the day her mother texted me with the answer and I left work to go home right away so that I could be there when Janine told Carissa. However, Janine wanted to make it an even bigger surprise, her mother said. She wanted to first tell Carissa that she wasn't allowed to go, and then in a couple weeks, tell her the truth when they exchanged Christmas gifts. How was I supposed to wait a couple weeks?! I am not a good liar, even when it is for a good cause, and thought there was no way I could keep the secret that long, but I agreed.

When I got home that afternoon, Janine and I gave each other a wink and when Carissa was out of the room we looked at each other with wide eyes both silently whispering "I'm so excited!." The girls left our house a few minutes later, Carissa dropping Janine off at her own house before she went on to cheer practice. A bit later, I texted Janine and told her to call me when Carissa wasn't with her anymore. When she called, she told me that Carissa knew that I had asked her mom because she had seen my phone a few days before, so she suggested I delete my messages. Good idea! I wondered how Carissa had seen my messages, but we keep our phones on the kitchen counter at our house at night so she may have inadvertently seen something without really meaning to. Or, she might have seen some old messages when we were in the car. I have a habit of handing her my phone when I am driving when I get a message or want to send one. Either way, I knew I would have to be more careful going forward.

Janine then told me her plan of texting Carissa later that night after cheer practice and telling her that her mom had said no, then giving her a gift of something like a picture of the Eiffel Tower in a frame, as part of her Christmas gift when they exchanged in a couple of weeks. I thought that was so sweet so of course I agreed to it. I also reasoned that Carissa couldn't say anything to me about Janine getting permission or not, without admitting that she had seen my messages, so I should be able to keep the secret without having a conversation where I had to lie or talk about it without giving everything away. I was covered!

As I had thought, Carissa never said a thing. The weeks slowly ticked by and finally it was the day for the gift exchange. I didn't know how I could find out exactly when the girls were exchanging that day without giving away the notion that something big was about to happen. I had lots of errands to run that day, it being the weekend before Christmas, so I set out to take care of those and hoped for the best that I would be home.

When I arrived back home, the girls had already exchanged their gifts so I missed the big reveal. It was just as fun, though, listening to the girls recount their story to me about the little gifts Janine included in the gift box as clues to the big gift, an Eiffel Tower tree ornament, mini-photo albums with French words on them, and a small travel journal. Carissa did not catch on. Finally at the bottom of the box was a homemade card stating "You really think I'd miss this lifetime experience? France 2017!" with a photo of the two girls and an image of the Eiffel Tower photoshopped into the background. Carissa teared up with the realization that this was really happening. Now we could really start planning!

Chapter 10

A Travel Companion For Myself

Now that each of my daughters had someone to travel with, I decided I needed a travel companion as well. One of my best friends, Marybeth, has always said that she would be up for a trip anywhere, anytime, so I immediately thought of her. Choosing someone to travel with is tricky endeavor though. It needs to be someone that you get along with *very* well, someone who is positive and upbeat, who is open to plans that can change on a whim, is organized, and not fearful of trying new things. Marybeth fit the bill for all of these qualities and more.

We had taken a few short weekend vacations together in the past, so I had been with Marybeth for extended periods of time, and had a feel for the way she approached vacations. We seemed similar in that aspect. We both liked to plan some parts of a trip out in an organized way, but we also were inclined to take time for relaxing and had no problem with adding downtime to our days.

There was still the part about the cost to contend with. Again, I had been saving for this trip for a couple of years so I was prepared, but would Marybeth want to spend a good chunk of money at one time like that? I wasn't sure.

We were at a Christmas party with friends during this time of considering and the topic of spring break vacations came up. Marybeth is a teacher, like me, so we tailor our vacations around our time off from school, which is typically during Christmas break, Spring break, or summer. Marybeth made it clear that she'd be willing to try any trip that anyone had an idea for. Her husband, Bill was currently working in a job that gave little to no time off during Spring Break or summer, so she especially noted that she would be willing to go on a trip alone if that was how the circumstances played out.

I decided to call her the next day. I started out my conversation with "I have something to ask you, it's kind of a big thing, so you can think about it and get back to me if you want." Then I asked if she'd be interested in joining me and the girls on our trip to France. Marybeth knew all about it, all of my friends did, since I had been planning it for so long. She was intrigued and excited about the proposition, but of course she wanted to discuss it with Bill and get back to me.

Her husband has a similar temperament to my husband, which is one reason why Marybeth and I understood each other so well as friends. Bill was easy going at times, but more likely to answer positively when he was in a good mood. Unfortunately, he had a hard day at work that night so she couldn't talk to him about it then. I understood, having been in the same position myself several times with Jeff. A few days went by and as I waited I started to think the answer might be no, and I imagined myself in France with the two teenagers all by myself. It wasn't a bad thought. The girls got along well and were pleasant to be around so I thought again, that I'd be fine with whatever the outcome would be, although I agreed with Carissa that it would be more fun with a friend for myself, than without.

Later that week, we had a surprise birthday party to go to that I knew I would see Marybeth at. I hoped she would have an answer for me there. We walked in and greeted our friends all around, and then inadvertently got seated at a table with another couple rather than with Marybeth and Bill. I didn't want to seem too eager for her answer so I figured she would come talk to me about it later.

The group walked to the area by the door of the party for the surprise for our friend, and as we were walking back to our table, Bill wrapped his arm around my shoulders and said, "Sorry, but I had to put the kibosh on your plan with Marybeth."

"Really?" I asked, looking up at him, "Why?" I knew that Bill, himself, had taken several trips alone with his friends, and although this trip was quite a bit longer and more expensive, I was still a little surprised that he was saying no to it.

"It's just not fair," he said. Then I *knew* he was kidding, he didn't think like that.

"No, you're kidding!" I exclaimed as I hit his shoulder and he burst out laughing. Of course she could go with me, he thought it was a great idea as well.

As we got back to the table, I told Marybeth that Bill had just told me the news. How exciting! Now we had quite the group going on this trip and I couldn't wait to get started planning it together.

Chapter 11

Travel Tips From Madame Seidler

In class during the spring, I asked my French professor Madame Seidler if she wouldn't mind giving me some tips when it came time to plan my trip. Of course she said yes, so in the fall before our trip I emailed her and we set up a day and time to meet at the local library to talk about my plans and see what suggestions she had.

First, I told her my initial plan, which was to go to Paris, then to a couple small cities, and then end in Nice.

"How long do you plan to be gone?" she asked in her beautiful French accent.

I told her, "About two weeks."

"Oh, bon bon!" she said "zat eez plenty of time." Good, I thought. I was wondering if that was too short or too long but had settled on about two weeks as a good amount of time to experience France myself. She also agreed with the initial plan and we began with talking about Paris. Since Madame Seidler was from Paris herself, I thought that this was a good idea.

So, Paris! Wow! This was really happening. I was finally sitting down to plan my trip to Paris, and with a real Parisienne, how cool! She asked me how I wanted to spend my time there. I told her that of course we wanted to see some of the major things like the Eiffel Tower, the Louvre and Notre Dame church, but other than that, we didn't want to do a lot of touristy things. We weren't interested in standing in long lines and we wanted to experience the "everyday Paris."

Madame Seidler gave me an overall view of the city and then she talked about the different *arrondissements*, or neighborhoods. I knew a bit about them and that they compared to the neighborhoods in Chicago where my daughter Rebecca lived. Those in Paris were numbered starting in the center of Paris and then spiraled out towards the outskirts. What I wanted to know was what each *arrondissement* was known for, where we should stay, and if there were any unsafe areas in Paris.

Madame told me that most of Paris is very safe, as safe as any big city can be. There were pickpockets and con-men that would take advantage of tourists but if we were sensible and mindful of our surroundings then we would be fine. She did warn me of the area around the Gare de Nord, and the 19th and 20th arrondissements. She said these areas have grown more rough in recent years and she recommended that we stay away from those. She said she herself took the subway near the Gare de Nord recently and she felt very uncomfortable, very unsafe. "Do not change trains at zee Chatelet or zee Montfunes Bienvenu, a nightmare!" she said. When I mentioned some of the terrorist events in Paris that have been in the news the past couple years, she explained that yes, that is the area where these have occurred and this is the area where there are some protests and uprisings so she tells everyone traveling to Paris to avoid those. She said the further west you go, the safer it is and the more refined. I didn't need any convincing.

Then we began to talk about where to go and where to stay. Madame took out her Michelin Guide and told me that this book is how she plans all of her trips home. The Michelin Guide publishes a list of hotels and restaurants recommended on a three-star award system. This guide has been published yearly since 1900 and establishments rely on this star system to boost interest from customers. This guide is very well respected. Madame believes that everything in this guide is worthwhile so it is a good place to find information.

These days when Madame Seidler goes to Paris, she rents a house outside of town and takes the train in everyday, but we wanted to stay right in Paris so we began looking at hotels there. She thought that if we took the train from the airport to the Gare de Lyon, then that would be a good place for us to stay. That is the student district so there would be a lot going on, and she began looking for a hotel for us within walking distance from the train station so that we wouldn't have to take a taxi when we got there and it would be convenient for when we left Paris for the next city. Taxis in Paris, she told me, cost too much money and besides that, they often wouldn't take more than 3 people because taxi drivers there do not allow people to sit in the front seat with them. Since we would have 4-6 people with us, having a hotel within walking distance seemed like a good idea to me too.

We looked up hotels in the Michelin Guide and she turned to the map and showed me exactly where each hotel would be and which way we would walk to get there. She would flip back and forth from the hotel section to the map as she explained other things about Paris hotels to me. Often, they came with a breakfast included, but that was usually optional. She said it could be pricey and she showed me how to find the price for each in the Michelin Guide. We found a few that she recommended and I wrote them down.

Next, Madame recommended some places and areas to visit. The Musee Montmartre was "delightful" she said. "Spend a day in that area." She told me to take the Jussieu subway, line #7 and get off at the opera house. Then take a taxi to Abesse street, to the Abesse church, then walk down Abesse street "Zere are lots of restaurants, and cafes zere. Do not walk down Anvers, eet ees too touristy. Zen, walk to zee left" she explained as she showed me on the map. " Walk down rue Tholoze, and end at zee Moulin de la Galette windmill."

The Moulin de la Galette was good, "a beet touristy though," Madame said. "After zat, turn right to rue Lepic." On that street she recommended many restaurants. Some Madame had visited herself, some she was plucking from the Michelin Guide naming how many stars each had been given and mentioning some of the descriptions about them in the guide. The Jeanne B, Le Coq Rico, Bistro Poulbot, I struggled to keep up as I wrote each of these down in my notes. I made a mental note to later borrow one of these guides from the library and to take the time to look up restaurants in there myself.

After covering Paris in depth, Madame began to tell me about some of the small cities that she thought would be nice for us to visit. She mentioned Amboise. I had never heard of that city before. "Very nice, very small, not too toureezty," she said. It is a small town in the Loire Valley that includes a chateau, farmers market, and good restaurants. Leonardo da Vinci spent part of his life here, which is part of the reason this village is frequented by tourists.

I mentioned to Madame the book Clochemerle and the city that inspired the author to write about it, Vaux-en-Beaujolais. I told her about how I had read about it in a magazine, gotten both versions of the book and even had the French copy with me to show her.

"Non!" she said "I have never heard of it. Not zee book OR zee city."

With that I thought, "Okay, I'll probably check that one off my list."

Another city she recommended was Beaune. It is middle sized, with *some* tourists but not too many. It is an old Medieval town. "When you go, you have to visit the Hospice de Beaune. Eet ees an old hospital, outside eet ees very dark, inside eet ees beautiful!" In 1443, Chancellor Nicolas Rolin founded Hotel Dieu (Hospice de Beaune) for the poor and most disadvantaged. She also talked about a small hotel called La Villa Fleurie that she had stayed in once. "Eet ees a short walk to zee center of the city, you will like it." Then she went on to talk about all that the city had to offer as to shopping, restaurants, etc.

With that, we began to wrap up. We had been at the library for several hours and I had taken about 6 pages of notes. I was exhausted and I hadn't even started planning the real trip yet. I thanked Madame Seidler profusely for spending so much time with me and giving me so many great ideas and suggestions. "A la classe prochaine!" we said, as we hugged goodbye, "Until the next class!"

Chapter 12

Creating My First Itinerary

After meeting with Madame Siedler, I sat down one afternoon to create my first itinerary for our trip. A few years back, I began getting several French magazines in the mail each month. Then over the last year, I had diligently flipped through every single back issue ripping out all that looked appealing to me. I chose everything from hotels, cities, and restaurants, to tours, classes, and travel tips. Anything and everything went into a French folder that I was keeping to organize my ideas for our trip.

That afternoon, I then began flipping

through all of the papers that I had saved in that folder. I pulled out all that still looked interesting to me and set aside things that I had changed my mind about, the city of "Clochemerle" being one of them. It was fairly easy to trim down my pile of articles now that I could actually picture myself in France. There were some tours in Paris that I still thought looked interesting. One article was for a shopping tour, an historical monument tour, or a foodie tour. Earlier when a friend asked me during this planning period, "What are you looking forward to the most?"

I answered, "Eating!", so of course I definitely kept the foodie tour part!

Lo and behold I could not believe my eyes when they came to rest on an article I had forgotten all about. It was for a cooking class in, of all cities - Beaune! The city that Madame Seidler had raved so much about. Could it be the same city? On closer inspection I saw that it was. This had to be providential. After Paris, we would travel to Beaune!

The cooking school sounded like a fascinating place. It is actually a cooking "studio" as they called it in the article, with a storefront where you can buy all sorts of items you might want or need in a French kitchen. I was picturing something like a Williams Sonoma or the cooking section of Bed, Bath, and Beyond. Then, in the back, the store boasted a classroom where they held cooking classes, and also meals for the students who signed up for the classes.

I pulled up the website for the studio online and the information there matched all that the article had mentioned and then some. This studio was started by an American mother and daughter some years ago. The daughter had married a Frenchman and moved to France and the mother didn't get a chance to see her much. She had always had a dream of opening a place that not only offered basic kitchen items and a knowledgeable staff, but cooking classes as well. At that point it was a time in her life that seemed like a good time to make her dream come true, so she moved to France to join her daughter and they opened the studio together - The Cook's Atelier.

There were several options on the website for cooking classes to choose from and I honed in on one in particular. It was a class called "A Day In Burgundy." This class was a little bit pricey but it sounded wonderful. First, you arrive at the local Farmers Market and along with the owners of The Cook's Atelier, you buy all of the food that you will be cooking for the day. Starting out with a stop at a flower stand to buy flowers for the dinner table, all the way to buying the meat, produce, cheese, bread and French wine bien sur!

Next, the website went on to describe that you would make your way back to the studio and learn how to cook all of the food that you just bought. Finally, you would sit down along with the hosts to eat all that you cooked and enjoy a long French lunch to cap off the day. The class would last from 10:00 am to 4:00 in the afternoon.

This sounded amazing to me! This would give us a spectacular thing to do in the city of Beaune. Not only would we be sightseeing, but we would be able to experience a typical French day of shopping, cooking, and eating and best of all, it would all be in English, which I thought was good since my French was still rudimentary and Marybeth and the girls didn't speak much French at all. This was starting out very positive.

After that, I flipped through the rest of the papers in my folder. I picked out a few more places to visit and things to do and began mapping out what each day would look like in France. From where we would go, to what we would do, leaving plenty of time for relaxing and sightseeing in between. I had a general plan all set. Now to take the next step and call the travel agent.

Chapter 13

Working with Travel Agents

During the summer before our trip, I talked with a friend at church who had gone to France a couple years ago with her son. She told me how she had gone to a local agency and for just $25, the travel agent had booked the whole thing for her including her flights, hotel rooms, and train tickets. She said the woman had been very helpful and had known exactly the type of tickets that would be best, and also the hotels that would be the best choice for her budget and plans.

I was excited to hear that, knowing

nothing about planning a trip myself, so I called the same agency and spoke to the same travel agent over the phone. I told her our preliminary plans and she told me that she would mail me some travel books and then in the fall I could make an appointment with her to come in and plan the trip.

The books she sent were beautiful but they were all group travel packages. I spoke to Carissa about it and she agreed that she was not interested in that kind of a trip. She had just gotten back from a group trip with our church to World Youth Day in Poland, and even though she had a wonderful time on that trip, she wanted to be more on our own than tied to the schedule, wants, and needs of a group. I had the opportunity to go to Rome sixteen years ago to take the place of a dear friend for a trip that was already paid for, with another church group and had the same experience. Even though that trip was an amazing one, I even got to see the Pope up close, traveling with a group was not what I wanted to do this time.

I emailed the travel agent in the fall, expressed our concerns about group travel, and attempted to make an appointment with her to plan our trip. She didn't get back to me for a couple of days, said she was booked that day, was off on Friday, and couldn't take an appointment the next week because her partner would be out of town. The only thing I could do was to try a walk-in appointment, although she couldn't guarantee that, since she would be the only one in the office. I was so disappointed. It didn't sound like she cared much about our business. I thought I would just have to look somewhere else.

I remembered that I had worked with another local travel agency when my two older children had gone on their spring breaks. The woman we worked with for those trips, which I went on with the kids, was very helpful. So, I called that agency and on the phone, again, the woman sounded very nice and helpful. Her name sounded familiar and I thought perhaps this was the same one we had worked with before. She asked me to send her an itinerary of what we wanted to do and then she would call me.

I had a day off of work a few days later so I sat down and diligently made an itinerary, then I emailed it to her. When she called me, she had a completely different tone to her voice. She sounded annoyed and said the itinerary I had sent couldn't be done. She mentioned several problems with it, such as no train to two of the cities I wanted to visit. I said I was surprised about that because I have a friend from Paris who told me that at least one of them for sure had a direct train, so I was confused. I had no idea of how planning a trip went and she seemed frustrated by that.

I think what I was expecting was that a travel agent would ask me what I wanted to do, find out the circumstances of my trip, such as this being a lifelong dream that I have saved diligently for, and not just a trip I was taking on a whim because I had extra money to burn. I also expected her to explain to me how planning a trip works, the choices that I had, and guide me as to how to work through them. She did none of that.

I asked her how much flights would cost from Detroit to Paris and she said she really couldn't say because they change all the time. I asked her if she knew of the cheapest airline to travel on and she didn't seem to have an answer for that. She mentioned Air France and the few other airlines that flew out of Detroit and said once we had a plan then she would have those prices.

I told her that we could be flexible and perhaps choose a different small city to visit after Paris. I asked her, "What do you recommend?"

She answered, "I have no idea."

I repeated back to her, "You have no idea? You have *no* recommendation?"

and she countered with "Well, you can come in and we can look at a map." I told her that would not help me. Looking at a map would give me no information about one French city from another, and that I had no idea of what would be a good place to visit besides what I already came up with. We agreed that we would get back to one another after I came up with another itinerary.

Later that night, I searched online for trains from Paris to the two cities that I wanted to visit, Beaune and Amboise. It is true, there was no train to Amboise, but there certainly was to the city of Beaune. I also looked up flights from Detroit to Paris and those from Windsor, Canada to Paris because I had heard that was an economical option, which I found to be true. I emailed her the links and the information that I had found. My husband was frustrated for me. He told me I was doing her work for her.

After a couple of days, the travel agent sent me an itinerary that she came up with. Yes, she agreed there was a train from Paris to Beaune after all. She put that on the itinerary, she had the flights from Detroit to Paris, she had a rental car in the package although I had told her I wasn't interested in driving, and she said it looked like the cooking school that I wanted to attend in Beaune wasn't taking reservations at this time. I was very frustrated. This was not at all what I wanted. I spent the week talking to several friends about traveling and how to book a trip by myself. Finally, I just emailed her back and said that my plans seemed to be changing, that I had a friend going with me who booked all her trips online by herself, and that I was going to have her plan our trip for us as well. I thanked her for her time and pledged to myself never to call her again.

Chapter 14

Planning with Marybeth: Two Heads Are Better Than One, Or So You Would Think

I had contacted Janine's Aunt Mary, a local French teacher that had lived in France for a while and she agreed to help us plan our trip, but before getting together with her, Marybeth and I sat down to plan our trip together one day. We wanted to be organized so that when we met with Aunt Mary, we had somewhat of an idea of where we wanted to go on our trip. So many people had told us that they had planned and booked their own trips themselves that we thought we could at least do the planning part and then Aunt Mary could help with the booking part. Our friend Kim told us at a Christmas party that she had booked all of her trips on Expedia.com and she found and reserved all of her hotels through the Marriott Hotel website. Another friend's daughter, Lindsay, explained to me at a wedding shower how she had booked all of her hotels, trains, and plane tickets in Europe with apps on her phone. How hard could it be? We thought if we were ready with our information, it would make it easier to plan with Aunt Mary.

Marybeth came over one afternoon and we began by looking up flights. We had been told that flying out of Windsor, Canada was cheaper than flying out of Detroit Metro Airport, which was the closest airport to us, so we started there. The amount of information was overwhelming. We weren't sure if we wanted to spend the money and leave closer to home, or if it was worth it to drive across the border to fly out of Canada. We also didn't know what to do first, book our flights, or book our hotel rooms? We talked and talked about the best way to go about this and then decided to wait on the flights and look at the hotels instead.

I shared with Marybeth the information that I had gotten from Madame Seidler about hotels and what to look for. We began looking up the hotels that Madame had suggested in Paris and Beaune. We also read about them on Tripadvisor.com. The information seemed good and informative but we were leery about choosing one until we knew more. We also looked at hotels in Nice, but couldn't tell which were good for the four of us and near the beach, which is what the girls wanted.

After 3 hours of looking at all of the information available online, we were no closer to planning the trip ourselves than before we had gotten together. C'etait tres difficile! We were overwhelmed and exhausted. We decided to call it a day and try again when we had a better idea of what we needed to do, and left it at that.

A few days later, we met with Aunt Mary and booked our hotels and flight tickets, that only left the train tickets for Marybeth and I to purchase on our own. Lots of people told us that they just bought their train tickets while in Europe on the days that they wanted to depart from one city to another. That might work for people who traveled to Europe often, but I wanted everything to go smoothly and Marybeth and I both thought it would be better to purchase them ahead of time if we were able.

So, on another day then, we looked up trains to the cities that we wanted to visit. We knew by then it would be Paris, Beaune, and Nice. We google searched "train tickets" to and from these cities. We could see that a train schedule existed but we could not figure out how to purchase the tickets. We put in the dates we wanted, and the options would come up but we couldn't seem to enter in our information and get the tickets. We tried over and over again putting in our departure dates for the TGV high speed train and the SNCF regular train but we couldn't get anywhere. We thought, "This cannot be happening again!" but we were bound and determined to get something accomplished that day. Finally we google searched "how to purchase train tickets in France" and as we read blogs and other websites for suggestions and answers, we found out that we couldn't purchase train tickets until 3 months in advance of the dates we were going to buy them for. That is why the ticket website would not accept our information when we keyed it in. So simple but you'd think there would have been some sort of information about this on the actual train ticket website itself. Done with what we could find out for the day, we went off to lunch.

When it was finally three months away from our trip, Marybeth and I sat down one more time to purchase our train tickets. We took out all of our papers and all of our plans and began looking online for our tickets. We knew we wanted the SNCF website but when we went to that site, and typed in "United States", it rerouted us to the Rail Europe website. There, we were able to put in all of our departure dates and search for tickets.

Marybeth meanwhile was looking over

our itinerary that she had typed and sent to me and Janine's mom to keep us updated on what was paid for and what our plans were. She had one note on there that questioned the departure date for our hotel in Beaune. I looked through the confirmation papers that I had printed from the hotel and all of the email communications with them and I didn't see that we had added one night to that part of our trip. We both remembered adding a night to one of the hotels but couldn't remember which one. I also looked through the papers that I had printed from the Nice hotel and kept referencing the second page that said we would arrive there on June 27, which is what Marybeth had on her itinerary. We looked over our calendar that we had written on and back at our papers and emails and then decided that we had forgotten to add a night in Beaune so I emailed the hotel to ask for an extension to our reservation.

Since we had double checked our dates, we thought we were ready to purchase our tickets. We wanted direct trains so that we wouldn't have to get on and off. We knew that with our sense of direction and limited language capabilities, getting on one train only was the best option for us. The only direct train to Beaune left at 7:00 in the morning. That was pretty early but we took it. Besides, that would get us to the city of Beaune at 4:00 in the afternoon and that was a good time.

Next, we looked at tickets from Beaune to Nice. There were no direct trains. Ugh! We really didn't want to change trains. Marybeth had just returned from Chicago and she and I both knew how confusing it was in that train station, reading and hearing everything in English, let alone being in a French train station. There was no other option though so we made the best choice according to time of departure and adding a TGV high speed train, so we chose the train going from Beaune to Chalon Sur Saone, and then from there to Nice. Again, we checked and double checked, and then put in our payment information and hit the "purchase tickets" button.

It was after I hit the button that I looked one more time at the cover page to the Nice hotel emails that I had printed off. On the first page was a note in French from the hotel stating that they were confirming our phone call to add one more day and that we would be arriving there on June 26 for our first night. June 26?? How did I not see this before?? I showed Marybeth and then we went over all of our papers, calendars, and itinerary again. Yes, we wanted 3 days at the beach in Nice, and 2 ½ days in the small city of Beaune but we had forgotten that or noticed it on our calendar until now. Oh la la!

We knew we would have to try and exchange our train tickets so we went *back* online to find out how to do that. There is a lot of information on the Rail Europe website but nothing really on how to exchange tickets. We knew there must be other people that made the same mistake we did. We found a live chat section and inquired on there as to what to do. The woman we chatted with told us that she could not help with exchanges and that we needed to call the 1-800 number so I called the number and were put on hold. We rolled our eyes and took a deep breath and then waited.

When I finally talked to someone, he was based in Chicago. He looked up our tickets and told us that we could not exchange them but that we would have to cancel them and then re-book the tickets. We would get 93% of our money back, and there would be a penalty fee. He didn't say how much. It was our only choice so we agreed and he went ahead and changed our tickets over the phone. We now had four new tickets, leaving at roughly the same time with the same transfer in Chalon Sur Saone. He said he would send us a confirmation email with the new ticket information and a breakdown of the extra fees. Great!

I still do not understand to this day with all of the checking and double checking, how we could have messed that up. At least we were problem solvers, something we teach our students to be, to not give up but to persevere until you've solved your problem. It probably helped that we had *no choice* but to persevere in order to get the right tickets on the right day.

They say "two heads are better than one" and I guess I would agree to some extent. If I had been doing this alone I would have been yelling at the computer, myself, and then crying before I solved the problem. At least with Marybeth here, we just cursed quietly under our breaths, questioned our sanity, and ended up laughing at the end.

Chapter 15

Planning with Aunt Mary

We scheduled a day over Christmas break for Janine's Aunt Mary to come over to our house with Janine and her mother, and Marybeth would be coming too. When Aunt Mary initially had heard that Janine would be going on this trip, she offered to help us plan with whatever we would need. Mary lived in France for a year in her 20's, had traveled herself a good deal over the years, and she teaches French at a middle school in Ann Arbor, Michigan, so she had a lot to offer us. I was so pleased.

I offered to have lunch for everyone for the meeting but I didn't know what to serve. What would be good but also easy for a small group? What would be something that everyone would like? I thought about pizza, maybe some salad...or picking up sandwiches, nothing sounded right. Finally, I had the perfect idea! I would make a charcuterie tray of cheese, crackers, olives and salami. How French! It would go perfectly with the theme of our meeting. I had picked up a very nice cheese board, bowls, mini forks, and cheese knives a few months earlier for another party and we had lots of cheese and crackers, and olives leftover from the holidays, including some good salami and cheese from a gift basket that we had received, so I didn't even need to go to the store, we had everything at home.

Aunt Mary and Janine arrived first. Aunt Mary is a big personality and she is quite tall. She has a very European classy look about her, and quite a presence. She entered the house with a burst of exuberance and "Bonjour! Bonjour!" with kisses on cheeks all around. "You have to know how to greet like the French!" she said as she gave us our first lesson in etiquette. One kiss on each cheek, but you don't really "kiss" the cheek as much as place your cheek next to each other and make a kissing sound. Carissa and I took their coats and offered our charcuterie tray on the coffee table as we waited for the others. "This is so beautiful!" said Aunt Mary. " I have to take a picture of it!" she said, as she snapped some photos with her phone. How sweet! I was silently glad that my choice for our meal went with our theme and met with Aunt Mary's French stamp of approval.

Marybeth and Janine's mother arrived and we got right down to business. Aunt Mary asked how this whole trip came about and I gave her the background story of how I was truly a Francophile, and that our house was not staged for her visit with our French magazines and books, or the Eiffel Tower on the mantel. Carissa corroborated my story. I explained how our group for traveling had grown from me and my daughters, to the group we had now. Aunt Mary thought that was lovely. She sat right down next to the coffee table and took out a fancy notebook to take notes on our trip.

Aunt Mary asked what we were all interested in doing on this trip. I went first, because I had a basic plan for the trip sketched out in my mind. We wanted to go to Paris, then to a small town, perhaps Beaune, then on to Nice and the beach to end our travels. Nice was Carissa's only request. Everyone agreed to this plan. We all wanted to see some tourist sights, like the Eiffel Tower and the Louvre, but we also wanted to have time for relaxing and just taking in the French culture. "I think that is a great idea,"-

said Aunt Mary. "You will find that the feel in Europe is very laid back, it is not like here, where we Americans go-go-go and the fact that you recognize this and want to enjoy that, is fantastic. C'est tres francais!"

We told her that we wanted to leave right after school ended for summer break and return for the 4th of July weekend back here in Michigan. We had one minor glitch and that was that Janine would have try-outs for a soccer team on the weekend we wanted to leave so that pushed our trip up to leave on Monday and because of the day I wanted to plan in Beaune, that had to be on a Saturday, that meant that we would have a shortened time than originally planned in Paris. There was some discussion of this and how everyone wanted more time in Paris so we suggested that perhaps we could turn our trip around and begin in Nice, then go to Beaune, then on to Paris for the majority of our stay. I left the room to get let the dog out, and get more water for everyone and when I came back in, they had all decided that Janine could miss the second half of tryouts, that she would email the coach, whom she knew personally, and get special permission, so that we could leave on Sunday after all. "What did I miss?" I asked, at this sudden turn of events, but somehow they had come to this conclusion while I was out of the room, so we went with it.

Next, we discussed why we wanted to go to Beaune, and Nice, because of course, wanting to go to Paris needed no explanation. I told everyone about how I came to know about Beaune from my French professor and from a magazine article, and Carissa explained that she didn't know why she wanted to go to Nice, she just did. She pictured herself and Janine on the beach in the south of France, and that sounded good to her. Aunt Mary then began to tell us what she knew of Nice, the good and the bad. The good: beautiful turquoise water, a quaint old part of the city called "old town" that we could explore, some good shopping, and people watching. The bad: rocky beaches, naked children on the beach and topless women in parts, very European, perhaps costly. We all suggested perhaps we should go to another part of France with beaches but Carissa and Janine would not be swayed. They really had their hearts set on Nice, so we all agreed, Nice it would be!

We then went on to talk about our traveling between cities. Aunt Mary suggested driving and Carissa and I looked at each other and smiled. There was no way I was going to drive in France, I could barely drive outside of our area here without getting lost. Then when I did get lost, more often than not, I would start to cry and that would not be good for anyone on this trip. I had a tendency of crying when I was stressed about driving, getting lost or having mixed up directions or plans. I knew that Carissa thought she would have "built in buffers" with Janine and Marybeth for any of that with me on this trip, I hoped she was right! We just laughed and explained all this to Aunt Mary and she agreed, driving was not for us.

And so, with that part in place, we began fervently planning. Five people all on technology of some sort looking for what we needed. Marybeth had brought her laptop so she began looking for flights. I had my laptop open so Aunt Mary and I began with that. Carissa had her laptop and began searching on her own. Janine and her mom had their smartphones.

We began with our hotel in Nice because we thought that would be the most difficult lodging to find. Locating a hotel on the beach proved way too pricey for our budget so we began to determine just how far we would be willing to walk with beach totes and such. Aunt Mary explained that there are few beaches that you can just walk down to from any hotel, and that we would need to pay for beach access daily. The cost would be about $20 a day and we all thought that would be fine and just part of our daily expenses.

We looked up one hotel after another and when we thought we had finally located one, Janine's mom called her phone provider to get the international plan temporarily, and then Aunt Mary asked, "Who would like to call?"

Of course I panicked, "Not me!" I said quickly and laughed. I feel like I know a fair amount of French but when called upon to speak it, my mind goes blank.

Carissa said "My mom knows more than me. If she can't do it, neither can I." So in the end, Aunt Mary agreed to be the official "caller."

It was so interesting to hear Aunt Mary speak with fluency on the phone in French! I could understand everything she said, I was just too nervous to make the call myself. Aunt Mary asked for a room for 4 people, and also asked about beach access. The woman on the phone told her that yes, they had a room for 4, and to get beach access, we would just need to walk a couple of blocks to the beach each morning. The cost of beach access was the same as Aunt Mary thought, about $20 a day. We had already located the hotel on the Google map so we knew that indeed it was only a few blocks away thus we agreed this was a good choice. The woman also mentioned that there was no view from our room of the Mediterranean, but we all profusely exclaimed, "That's okay, that doesn't matter," because we didn't plan to be in our room much but out enjoying the Mediterranean in person.

So, we booked the room. Immediately, my phone rang. It was the bank! I was booking most of our trip through my debit card because I was the one who had money saved up in the bank and was ready to go. I didn't realize I would have to let the bank know already that I was spending money for the trip, but it made sense since the card was charged in Nice and not here in the US. I explained the situation and also explained that I would have several more transactions that day. Lesson learned.

After Nice, we were on a roll. Marybeth had found several options for flights. For us, it was cheaper to drive to Canada and leave from Windsor, rather than Detroit, so we looked at those choices. All of the flights had layovers so we weighed the pros and cons of each layover, and also looked at the arrival times, not wanting to arrive in the dead of the night in a foreign city. At last, we found a flight that met all of our criteria. "Ok, hit the button," said Aunt Mary. We were hesitant, but she said, "All you need to do is make the decision." So with all of us looking over her shoulder, Marybeth hit the button and we were booked! Four flights to Paris, France, return flights from Nice.

We breathed a sigh of relief, "Whew!" and high fived all around.

We moved on to Beaune. I had a hotel suggestion from Madame Seidler, my French professor, so that would be easy. We pulled it up on the computer and checked the walking distance to the cooking studio (I found out later that for our cooking class we were to meet at the market, not the studio, but it was still good to be in the same proximity for our hotel). The place looked lovely! La Villa Fleurie. We all agreed to it so Carissa filled out the online booking form and hit send. We got back a very nice note that informed us that the family that ran the Bed and Breakfast (for that was indeed what it was), was "on holiday" and that we could only "pre-book" our room. They would get back to us at their earliest convenience to confirm our reservation. Aunt Mary continued our education as to how laid back the French were and that this was, "Pas de probleme!", "Not a problem."

Finally, Paris! We thought this would be the easiest city of all to find a hotel in. First of all, I had a recommendation from Madame Seidler for a hotel. When we looked it up however, the cost was out of our price range. Also, this hotel was near the train station, the Gare de Lyon. Madame Seidler suggested that would be a good location so that we wouldn't have to walk far with our luggage when we took the train to Beaune. However, Aunt Mary advised that it was not a wise idea to get a hotel near a train station in general. That it wasn't as safe as other areas, and that the clientele could be less than savory. We were all ears. We would look for one wherever she suggested. She suggested the St. Germain area. It was a quaint area, very typical Parisian, and a nicer part of Paris, she believed. We looked it up on Google images and it did look so sweet and quaint that we all put our energy into looking for a hotel in that area instead. I realized that some of the travel tips from Madame Seidler were just recommendations and we'd have to use only the suggestions that worked for us.

There were several factors that I didn't take into account before. First of all, Paris hotels were very expensive. I thought there would be more moderate to cheaper priced ones but there weren't. Aunt Mary suggested a hostel where you share rooms with others that you don't know and we all said "No!" in unison, laughing out loud.

"Okay, no then," smiled Aunt Mary. She knew then that a hostel was not the right vibe for traveling for this group.

Another thing that I had forgotten about was the fact that Paris hotels do not all include an attached bathroom. Often, guests have to walk down the hall to bathrooms shared with other guests. While, truly, that would not be the end of the world, and a bit of "roughing it" would be fine with me, kind of like living in a group dorm with a shared bathroom, having the young girls have to use a shared bathroom while on this trip did not sound safe to me so we all vetoed that option as well.

Next, we had to contend with the fact that most Paris hotels only have room for two people. Who knew? Finding one for four proved to be very difficult. Even with all five of us on technology searching and searching, we were coming up short. We decided to up our budget from what we were willing to spend, and to search for "family" hotels. Even with that, the options were limited and we found online advice that said those hotel rooms were few and far between in Paris. Aunt Mary called a few places asking for "une chambre pour quatre personnes" but her effort was less than fruitful. Then Janine's mom found one while searching on her smartphone. We discussed it quickly and then clicked on the reserve button immediately. We got it! It was a room for 4, with an attached bathroom, in the St. Germain area and only $50 over our budget per night.

We sat back, happy with our accomplishment. We still had a few minor details to attend to on another day but for now, our main parts of the trip were booked and we were thrilled.

Chapter 16

French Language CD's From the Library

I am a big fan of the public library. It started when I was a little girl and my mother took me and my four brothers and sisters to the library every week to get books. I still remember when I got my *own* library card, and signing my name while standing at the very important front desk. I loved walking down the aisles and taking time to choose carefully what I wanted to read each week. I found the card catalog fascinating. It was so organized and had a card for *every* book in the library. I remember walking up to the huge chest of little drawers and opening one to flip through the cards in search of the one for the book I was looking for. I couldn't believe that we could check out "as many books as we wanted" and often took home as big a stack as I could carry. When my own children were growing up, we visited the library every week as well. Not having much money as a young family, this was the best way for me to be able to get books to read to them each night and as they grew, they also enjoyed going, getting their own library card and choosing their own stack of books.

I'm always amazed at how few people take advantage of not only borrowing free books at the library, but all of the other free services as well. The magazines, movies, games for children, internet service, newspapers, etc. One day while I was there it occurred to me, French language tapes! I had seen these in the bookstore, so why not in the library? Then I remembered that one of the women in my French Conversational Class had mentioned learning from language tapes. I walked over to the tapes and CD section and there, down low, on a shelf under the book club sets of books, there were language CDs for nearly every language you could think of. Of course! Why hadn't I thought of this before? Now I could listen to the CDs in my car on the way to and from work and fit in even more practice on a daily basis. Even though my commute was only 10 minutes each way, that added up to 20 minutes more a day, which I felt would be "using my time wisely" as I always teach my students to do.

I looked over both of the two CDs that I saw there for French. One was by itself, and one came in a three CD set. Although I checked out both, I decided to start first with the one that was by itself. It looked pretty old, but I was already looking forward to popping the CD in my car come Monday morning on the way to work.

The first segment came on saying, "First lesson: greetings and farewells," *"Premiere lecon: salutations et adieux."* The lessons would follow the format of listening to the speaker on the CD and then repeating. This, the instructor said would be "Like a child learns his native tongue." Each sentence, or phrase, would be given in English, followed by the French. Then there would be a pause that would give me time to say the phrase out loud.

As it got going I knew the first few ones bien sur, but I always start a new French study program at the beginner level. It helps me to think that I've made progress over time and re-enforces what I've already learned. I figured I would fly through the first few lessons. I even tried to predict what the answer was and say it before the instructor, "Good Morning," he said.

"Bonjour!" I thought to myself.

"Bonjour."

"Good Evening."

"Bon Soir!"

"Bon Soir." etc. I was feeling good.

What was this however? Yikes! Only the first lesson and already there were phrases I didn't know. "What is the matter?" the instructor said next.

"Hmmm...", I thought.

"Que y'a t-il?"

" I hope that she feels better soon."

"J'espere...no idea!"

"J'espère qu'elle va mieux bientôt." Huh?

"Oh," I moaned inside my head, "Really? How do I not know what he is saying?" I decided to just keep listening and repeating.

"In no time," the instructor promised, "you will be amazed at how quickly you will be speaking French." Ok, I was in it to win it, I would do this, I would listen and repeat every day. That's why I got these in the first place, right? I asked myself. I was just disappointed that I couldn't recall the French words as quickly as I thought I should be able to by now. But this would be good for me, just one step closer to my "getting to Paris" and I buckled down and paid attention so that I could master this as well.

As the weeks went by, the French tapes helped considerably. I began to memorize the other phrases as well. I had knowledge of the words but I just couldn't recall them very quickly. If I heard them or read them, I usually knew them, but to come up with them on my own was challenging. With practice, I got better and better.

I returned the first CD set to the library and decided to try the next one. This set had three CDs and three books included. I took the first CD in the car and popped it in. Ugh! This was not what I was looking for at all. It simply spoke, in French, word after word, as though reading a list. The CD did not translate any of the words at all. I decided to just keep listening and try to guess at the words and then repeat them as well. I did this for a few days and then I got out one of the books and flipped through it trying to figure out the format. It seemed like it was meant for a student to read the book along with the CD. The translations were in the book. I obviously couldn't do this in the car, so I decided to return this set to the library and re-check out the other one. That, and I would perhaps visit some other local libraries and check out some different language CDs from those as well. It certainly couldn't hurt and then I would definitely be "using my time wisely."

Chapter 17

——

Conversational French Class, the Second Time

I was thrilled and still a little nervous to go back to my conversational French class a second time. Would I understand more this time? Would I be able to participate better? Would I still be as nervous? All this and more I was thinking in the days and weeks leading up to my first class for the Fall term.

Madame Seidler teaches for ten weeks a term, one in the fall until just after Thanksgiving, one in the winter leading into the first weeks of spring, and one in the springtime. Her reason for only these three terms being that her students are busy with their own lives, especially during the holiday season and summer, and are too busy to attend class. Also, being a native Parisienne herself, she travels back to Paris every summer for a long stay, so she doesn't teach class in the summer either.

I started taking this class only nine months ago, when I realized I wasn't improving my French by having our French student living with us. This would be my second term with this group of people also learning the language, and yet, it felt like it had been much longer. This group was such a nice, friendly, welcoming group of women and men, that I thought of them somewhat as friends rather than just other students in a class.

I had studied on my own a fair amount over the summer break so I felt somewhat prepared. I continued to do my Duolingo lessons nearly every day, I had listened to

Coffee Break French a lot, and studied my notebook and other French lesson books. When I went back to class on the first day, it was a welcome sight to see Madame Seidler and all of my friends again.

As I sat there I realized that yes, I was able to understand more of what was being said. I even joined in the conversation myself a few times the first day, which was a major accomplishment for me. The women in the class talked about what they had done over the summer, where they had vacationed, and how their families were doing. It was a very nice conversation, tout en francais.

We then discussed what we did for work. I learned how to ask what someone did and how to answer with what I do, "teach third grade", "J'enseigne la troisieme niveau." There were several "stay at home" women in the class, they seemed to come from money and mostly talked about traveling and entertaining and such. Other women in the class had careers. One woman in the class was an artist, she created things at home and sold them in a studio. Another woman was a lawyer. Another was a recent college graduate looking for a career in French, and one woman was a college art professor and also a museum docent.

I found these women fascinating. I talked to the woman who was an artist a bit. She had been on a recent trip to France with her husband and friends. She was a member of a group called "Jews for Jesus." This is a group of people that were Jewish, but then had converted to Christianity. She told us, in French, that she had gone to France on a mission trip over the summer. She and her group had gone essentially to evangelize to Jews there about the good news of Jesus Christ and to share their conversion story. I am always interested in evangelization and how people go about it so I was curious about how she went about this and what the reaction of the French people she talked with was. In essence, she said that her group was not received well at all. They tried to evangelize outside of certain Synagogues that they knew of with pamphlets and by talking to the people. They were treated with rudeness and disdain. I'm sure it was difficult for her and the others, she did not seem happy with the outcome. Still, I was impressed with the fact that they not only tried to share what they felt in their hearts, but also that they did it in another language.

Another woman that I talked to was the museum docent, college art professor. She also had visited France over the summer but she had gone by herself. I was curious about how and why she traveled by herself. She explained that in the past when she had traveled with friends, she had ended up spending most of her time talking in English with them. She intended to speak mostly in French this time, hence the fact that she did not travel with anyone who would distract her from that. Since I also had a goal of speaking French while on my trip, I wondered how she had spoken much French when she was just a typical tourist, that being my concern as well. She said that she had to push herself out of her comfort zone and talk to people in the course of her everyday activities. She spoke to museum docents when she visited museums, she spoke to waiters and waitresses at meal time, and she struck up conversations with strangers in coffee shops, on park benches, etc. She did admit that she had to be a bit careful at times about this because the European men sometimes took this friendliness as flirting and she was not interested in that at all. All in all, she offered very good advice!

As we were talking about summer vacations, one woman played some French music on her smartphone and we discussed music and everyone's favorite type. Madame Seidler began going around the room asking each person, in French, what they liked and why and to give some examples of musicians or singers they liked. I began preparing in my head what I would say, even as I listened to the others. I did fine when it was my turn and was able to answer that I mostly listened to jazz and classical because they were quiet, relaxing types of music and after teaching my class of eight year olds all day, I enjoyed peaceful music afterwards. Other women shared a variety of music that they enjoyed as well.

After this topic of conversation, Madame Seidler asked us students to volunteer to bring in something to share with the class, or come up with a topic each week that we could use as a basis for our conversations. The college graduate volunteered for the next week and she brought up "movies" so we had a lively conversation about our favorites in both English and French. I volunteered for the following week. I always try to volunteer early when it comes to presentations, otherwise my nervousness builds along with the anticipation of my turn. Even though I was feeling more comfortable, I wanted to get my turn over with.

At home, I looked through my French magazines for a topic of interest that I thought would lead to a good conversation for the class. I was aiming for a bilingual article so that I could know exactly what it was saying, since I still felt a little under water during some of the conversations in class. I found a nice article all about plays and broadway type shows so that was our topic for conversation. We read the article out loud in French together, and then we spoke about what broadway shows we had seen and which ones were our favorites. I had seen *The Fiddler on the Roof, The Phantom of the Opera,* and *Annie* but my absolute favorites were *Wicked* which I had seen three times, and of course *Les Miserables* which I had seen twice as had all of the other students in the class. It was a good conversation and one I could follow well. I was relieved that my turn for volunteering was over and excited to see what everyone else chose for their topics in the coming weeks.

All in all, the class went very well. There were many topics that we discussed that interested me and I could keep up with the basic vocabulary of them.

At the end of this term, Madame Seidler invited us all to bring an appetizer or dessert dish and have a party again on the last day. I wanted so badly to make something

French so I began looking up recipes online. I found a great, easy recipe for olive tapenade on baked, buttered, baguette. I brought it in the night of the party and was so proud of myself because the French Chef was back as our guest this time and after he tasted my dish he asked, "Who made this?" and when he found out it was me said, "C'est tres delicieux!" What more could I ask for?

Chapter 18

Private Lessons with Aunt Mary

After meeting with Aunt Mary to plan our trip, I decided to ask her if she would consider giving me private French lessons. My conversational class was going well, but I felt that I needed one-on-one lessons to push myself to talk more. I texted Aunt Mary and she agreed so the following week we met for our first lesson.

Aunt Mary lives in a quaint area of Ann Arbor, Michigan called Kerrytown. She chose to live there because it is very similar to the area of Paris where we were going to be staying on our trip, St. Germain. She had visited that area when she was in Paris years ago and loved the look and feel of it. Like St. Germain, Kerrytown has lots of small shops and restaurants. It has a Farmers Market and lots of outdoor space for gathering with others in the community.

On my first drive there I was a little nervous. I had never been to this part of town before. I didn't know if it would be difficult to find or hard to park there but I was willing to give it a shot. I diligently followed my GPS and easily found the neighborhood and began looking for my parking options on the small city side streets. Many streets had meters and Aunt Mary had told me about those so I had brought change. We had agreed to meet at a coffee shop and luckily I found a parking spot right outside of it. It was parallel parking but I had no problem. I had aced parallel parking in driver's ed class in high school, something I'm still proud of, even though I can rarely use this skill in my suburban life.

I went inside and found the coffee shop very similar to a Starbucks with a cozy, homey atmosphere, but not quite as quiet. I thought that might be good so that no one would be wondering why we two were talking in French, my French not even being that good. I bought a soy latte and began looking for a table when I got a text from Aunt Mary. She was walking over from her nearby apartment and recommended that I find a table in the courtyard. It was one of those beautiful days in late winter/spring in Michigan where the weather was balmy and the sun was out so a courtyard seat was perfect!

I was able to find a table and sat down with my coffee. I was already feeling very French because it felt just as though I were at an outside cafe in Paris. The sun was shining, and there was just the right amount of shade. The table and chairs were made of simple black wrought iron, very classic and Parisian I thought I could sip my coffee and people watch as I waited for Aunt Mary.

When she came around the corner, we hugged, and kissed on the cheek, just as the French do and she of course greeted me with a "Bonjour!"

I was ready with a "Bonjour!" back and I followed up with, "Comment ca va?" "How are you doing?" We chatted like that for a minute and then sat down to get to work.

After I paid Mary, we talked about the lessons and she asked me how I would like the lessons to go and the goals I had for them. I explained to her that basically I wanted to just have conversation and that I wanted her to help me along to think of words and be able to come up with what I wanted to say. I explained to her my background in the language, and all of the types of lessons I'd had in the past. I told her that I felt that I knew a lot of words and grammar in my head but one problem was, I couldn't think in French very fast and I had a difficult time coming up with what I wanted to say when put on the spot, and two,was that I was very shy about speaking in French and so when it came time to use what I knew, I would just clam up.

I explained to Mary some examples of my shyness and inability to speak French when I wanted to. Once, when my daughters and I were at Epcot Center in Florida at the Around The World exhibit in the France section, my daughter Rebecca tried to get me to speak French to the workers there. I couldn't think of a thing to say! I couldn't remember how to say anything besides "bonjour" and I didn't want to start with that and then not have anything to say to follow it up.

As we stood in line for a lemon ice, I couldn't think of how to order it or even the word for lemon. I was so frustrated with myself. My daughter and I just laughed though and ordered in English like everyone else and kept on walking down the way. It wasn't until about 20 minutes later as we were walking that I thought of all *sorts* of things to say. I remembered how to say "How are you? I am doing well; Please may I have a lemon ice cream? Where are you from? We are going to have a French student live with us next year," etc. I wanted a "do over" but by then we were far from the France section of Epcot.

I told her of another time, when the French Chef was cooking for our French class and I was helping out in the kitchen. He began asking me in French to get him this or that, how I liked cooking, if I liked the kinds of food he was preparing, and if I knew how to do the prep work that he was asking me to do. I totally clammed up again. I could only force out "oui" and "non." I felt really pathetic but again, what could I do but laugh about it? So I did and went on to enjoy the night determined to be better prepared the next time.

So now was my chance, with these private lessons to be better prepared for my trip. Mary understood all of this and more. She explained that everyone feels like that when they are learning the language and the fact that I kept trying and working hard at it was the important part. She took out a few books and a workbook and showed me some things in them to help me. We then began to talk in French.

Mary did a wonderful job of putting me at ease and talking to me about many things that I knew the vocabulary for and could stumble my way through the grammar for. When I forgot a word in French, I could ask her in English what the equivalent was, and she helped me through that and also showed me how to look it up on the app on my smart phone with Google Translate. I was used to looking things up on the Google Translate website but hadn't thought of using my phone for that before.

At the end of our first lesson, Mary said she was impressed with how much French I knew. I don't think she was expecting me to know as much as I did. Now the only trick was being able to recall it with others as I did with Mary.

After that first day, we began to meet every other week at the coffee shop. We sat down each week and talked casually about all of the everyday things in our lives, which was exactly what I was looking for. Since we were both teachers, we shared how our weeks went with our students, our colleagues and our administrators. We shared news about our families and fun we had with our friends. Mary was then dating another teacher from her school and was even planning a trip to France herself with him the summer I was going on my trip as well.

Mary shared with me some French items that she had. One was a book of many historic restaurants in Paris. I took it home, read it, and really studied the restaurants in the 6th arrondissement, St. Germain. It was very interesting and really amazing that there were these restaurants with such a rich and timeless history. I couldn't wait to visit them on our trip.

Another thing Mary shared with me was a boxed set of Paris walking tour cards. They were all set up to take a tourist around different areas and arrondissements, each being about an hour in length of time it would take to complete one. It gave notes on sights to see in each area such as shopping, old churches, historic sites, etc. Mary explained to me that one card in particular had an ink outline around one particular area where her friend who had given her the set of cards, had visited. This area that she had drawn on the card was the most authentically French area, she shared. In the spot there were restaurants and shops that the Parisians themselves ate and shopped at, and the area that was the least touristy. I took the set home and immediately found that card. I planned to take the set with us so that each day we could decide what we wanted to do, and especially to visit the area that was outlined by Mary's friend.

I shared with Mary some French things of my own as well. I shared with her some articles that I had saved over the years about France. I also shared with her my two books about the French city of Clochemerle, the one in English and the one in French. I figured she would have more luck than I did reading the French one. We also shared French movies that we'd seen and gave each other advice about other French books we had read. We began to become more than just teacher and student, we began to become friends, and this made these lessons more enjoyable than I ever imagined.

Chapter 19

Building Anticipation

I love to build anticipation with my family, friends, and students whenever I am planning something big. I believe that anticipation is part of the fun of enjoying anything worthwhile. It makes the planning stage enjoyable and exciting. At school, I will drop hints to my class or write "secret surprise" on our calendar about upcoming events or visitors to my classroom. With my friends, I will talk about events that we are going to do together, getting them to become excited before the events come up. In my family, I text, leave notes, and have conversations about adventures that are coming up in order to build anticipation for them as well.

For this trip, in the spring before we left I decided I wanted to do some special things for the girls as we looked forward to our trip. I began researching online for creative ideas to help build these intriguing feelings. I read blogs, posts, and articles about families and friends and how they went about building interest for their trips and events. I was looking for anything that I could do simply and inexpensively. I looked for small gifts and countdown ideas. I didn't see much about traveling countdowns except for traveling to Walt Disney World, there were many of those! Some were quite adorable as families worked to get their children excited about their vacations there. Who wouldn't be excited about that? The build up with a countdown was just icing on the cake.

I'm not that crafty these days, having used up all of my creativeness when my children were young I think. Because of this, I was looking to "copy" something, not come up with something of my own. I searched and searched for a countdown to a trip to Paris and came up short with nothing. Some posts suggested apps on smartphones for countdowns but I wanted something tangible. Years ago, I helped Carissa make a wedding countdown on a large presentation board for a dear friend of ours. I was looking for something like that for our last thirty days.

In the meantime, our trip was three months away. I decided to send a photo to each of the girls once a week for a month, to begin the build up to our trip. The first Saturday, while I was having coffee with my husband, I looked up pictures online of Paris and found the perfect picture of the Eiffel Tower. I sent it to Rebecca, Carissa, Janine and Marybeth with a note saying

"Good Morning ladies! Three months from today and we'll be leaving for Paris!" They all responded back with excitement. A week later, I sent a picture of an adorable outside cafe with a note, in French this time "Bonjour mes amies! Ici est un petit photo pour vous d'un café en Paris." I figured they could figure out the simple French or at least translate it with Google. "Hello my friends. Here is a small photo for you of a cafe in Paris." The third week it was a picture of a breakfast of croissants and coffee in delicate cups, on a beautifully set table on a terrace, with a view of the Eiffel Tower in the background. Again in French, my note read " Bonjour! Peut-être nous aurons un petit-déjeuner comme ca pendant que nous somme a Paris!" I admit I used Google translate myself to make sure I had the correct grammar for this one. "Good Morning! Maybe we will have a breakfast like this while we are in Paris!" Lastly, I sent a photo of the Louvre museum since we would be visiting there on our trip. This time in English I wrote "Two months until our trip! This is the Louvre museum, can't wait to visit it while we're there!" Each time I sent these texts, the group all responded back with excited texts themselves. I felt like we were all starting to feel the anticipation.

For the next month, I wanted to buy the girls one small gift a week. I began looking in stores. Originally I was going to mail Rebecca her gifts in Chicago but that proved to be too much for me, so I just sent her pictures of the things I was giving to the rest of our travel group instead. The first week, I bought French cookies, macarons, at a local store. I bought each young girl cookies in their favorite color, pink for Janine, blue for Carissa. I then bought yellow for Marybeth and I included some for Aunt Mary as well because it was her birthday that day. I bought four for each person and had the baker wrap each group of four in individual boxes. I then went home and wrapped each little white box in ribbon and added notes about this being a "little something" to get them excited for the trip. The second week, I found pencil sets for each person. These were adorable sets that I found at a specialty paper store in Ann Arbor while shopping with Aunt Mary after class one day. The case was a light pink and cream shade with silver edges and inside were 8 pencils covered in paper of the same shades and a sharpener. Both the pencils and the case were covered with French words, and pictures of the Eiffel Tower. I wrapped each one in tissue paper and added a note about them using the pencils at school and each time they did, they would think of our trip! The third week, I found some little tissue packages with a picture of the Eiffel Tower and a girl with a red umbrella. I wrapped them in tissue paper again and dropped one off at each house. Lastly, I bought a pack of four French magnets. I opened the pack and separated the magnets into individual tissue paper packages and dropped those off as well. I told the girls they could put the magnets on their locker at school or on their refrigerator at home and hopefully whenever they looked at it, they would think of our trip. Each of these were just a little something to get everyone excited. Marybeth was so sweet though, she texted me later one day after receiving her last gift and said "even though you say these are little things, they mean alot to me" and I was so happy they did.

I worked hard to come up with a countdown for the last month before our trip. Since I didn't find anything online, I knew

I would have to come up with something myself. I took some ideas from the numerous Disney world countdowns I saw and decided to create a countdown on scrapbook paper with stickers and put it in an 8 x 10 picture frame that could be set on a table. On the glass part of the frame, each person could write the number of days left before our trip with a black wet-erase marker, and then wipe it off each day in order to change the number.

I had to create Rebecca's first because she was going to leave about 10 days before us. I also wanted to mail her gift to her in Chicago so I had to plan ahead for shipping time. I went to Michael's craft store and began by looking at the picture frames. I wanted ones that would stand up so they needed the back part that would prop them up. Luckily they had some very simple black 8 x 10 frames on sale, so I bought four, for about $5.00 each.

Next, I went to the scrapbooking section of the store. I wanted the super fancy 3D stickers. I was looking for travel ones and I knew I had seen ones with the Eiffel Tower on them before so I kept an eye out for those. For Rebecca's, I wanted to create a part on the countdown for each of the three cities that she would be visiting, London, Barcelona, and Paris. I couldn't believe my luck when I found the most beautiful 3D sticker sets for each of those three cities.

The sticker set for London had a palace guard, a red phone booth, a double decker bus, a crown and the British flag on it. The one for Barcelona had the church of the Sagrada Familia, a flamenco dancer, a bull, and a guitar. For Paris, the set included the Eiffel Tower, the Arc de Triomphe, a metro sign, a cup of "cafe", and a croissant with a French flag sticking out of it. Each set also had a beautifully designed name plate for the famous cities. I took each set and carefully placed it was displayed in the package, onto a piece of beige cardstock. I then laid these out onto an intricate piece of scrapbook paper with a subtle dark beige Fleur de Lis design. At the top I added the words, "Countdown to our trip!" along with a heart sticker with an airplane on it that was printed with "adventure awaits." I placed this in the frame and then wrapped up the whole thing with the black marker and a note about changing the number of days until her departure every day until she left. I mailed it out the next day, texted Rebecca to watch for it in the mail and then waited.

She texted me as soon as she got it. She loved it! She couldn't wait to share it with her roommates and her boyfriend. She wanted to share it on social media but I asked her to wait until I gave Carissa and

Janine theirs because they follow her on her sites and I didn't want them to know about the surprise.

Two weeks later, I woke up early on a Saturday and began working on the rest of the countdowns. I was going to make three more, one for Janine, one for Marybeth, and one for Carissa and I to share. For these I just used a set of Paris stickers for each one and with the design of the paper, they still looked just as cute.

I gave Carissa hers in the morning when she woke up. I had wrapped it in tissue paper so she unwrapped it and then gave me a big hug. We set it up in the living room on a side table so that we could see it every day when we walked past it. I texted Janine to see if she was home and she was at the gym but promised to stop by our house afterwards. She came in for a quick visit when she got here and I gave her the gift, she loved it. Next I drove over to Marybeth's house and gave her hers. I told her this was my last gift but it would last her for a month. She loved it too! She even thought about how she could use it after the trip by adding photos of our adventures and just covering up the words about the countdown. I was so glad I had come up with an idea that everyone could use to get excited about the trip. Now to just make it through the next thirty days!

Chapter 20

Getting to Paris – Literally (Car, Planes, and a Taxi)

The day was finally here! I had planned, saved, organized and packed. Now the time had come when I would truly be 'getting to Paris!'

It had been a really busy week at work. It was our last week of school and since most of our lessons were finished by this week, we had to do extra work to keep the students occupied during the last few days. On top of that, our school was being rearranged over the summer so I had to pack up my entire classroom and move it to a new classroom and be done by Friday afternoon, the same day as the last day of school for students. The next day, Saturday I packed all day, and then we were scheduled to leave the following morning.

I didn't think I would be able to sleep well the night before but thankfully I did. Of course I woke up early before the alarm though and began to get ready. I woke my daughter, got dressed and gathered my things in a bit of a haze. It still didn't feel real to me.

We began getting texts from our friends Marybeth and Janine that morning. Everyone was excited to go. Janine's mom even took a picture of her with her countdown filled in with '0 days!' written on it.

We left our house early by car at 6:45 a.m. My husband had offered to drive us to the airport. It was about thirty minutes away. We were too excited to eat so we planned to have breakfast at the airport once we checked in. We had to say good-bye to our golden doodle dog, Ozzy. We knew he would wonder where in the world we were over the next two weeks. Carissa gave him a big hug and kiss, explained everything to him, and then headed out the door. We checked and double checked that we had everything, especially my husband's passport to get into Canada, then Jeff loaded our luggage in the car for us and we were set to go.

We only left a few minutes late than our planned departure from our house. We got to Marybeth's first. She had her suitcase sitting on her front porch. "Bonjour!" she said as she came out the front door.

"Bonjour!" we all replied back. A kiss and a hug goodbye to her husband first, then Marybeth climbed into the car and we took off. It was to Janine's next. She came out with her mom. Again, we checked that she had everything. In addition to her passport, she had a notarized letter from her parents giving her permission to travel with us. Finally, we were on our way. I was 'getting to Paris' as I'd been wanting and planning to, for so long.

As we drove to the border between Detroit and Windsor, Canada we all began to get a little nervous. I'm not sure why, but talking to border guards always makes me feel this way. We instructed the girls on how to act and what to say. We explained that we weren't allowed to answer for them. We told them to roll the window down in the back seat, sit up, and answer whatever questions were asked of them by the border guard. They felt fine with all of our directions but still slightly apprehensive.

We got to the border and everything

went smoothly. The guard asked for our passports, asked where we were going and why, matched up the photos on our passports with each of us and sent us on our way. Down the road we laughed at our unnecessary nervousness and that he didn't question us having Janine with us even though she had her parent's letter ready to hand him just in case.

Driving to the airport then proved to a bit of a problem. Once we went over the border, none of our phones would connect to the internet for data. We were so used to using GPS for directions that we didn't have a paper map with us to find out how to get to the airport. We knew it was only twenty minutes away but we had no idea in which direction it was! My husband then got directions the old fashioned way, by rolling down the window of his truck and asking someone who was walking by on the sidewalk. The girls thought that was the funniest thing but we had no other choice. By following this person's verbal directions, we got to the Windsor airport in no time.

We pulled up to the front door of the Windsor airport and jumped out, eager to get our suitcases and check in. For some reason I had the most luggage of all! We each had one large suitcase to check and then one bag to carry. Marybeth and the girls had backpacks and I had my work bag, similar to a briefcase in size and shape. I also had a small carry-on suitcase. This small suitcase turned out to be a hassle the whole trip. I had all my shoes, and heavy things in it. I'm used to packing that way so that my clothes don't get wrinkled by those items. Hindsight being 20/20, I should have just fit those heavy things in my big suitcase.

I had thought carefully about my traveling outfit. I knew it would be a long day and I wanted to be comfortable so I opted for leggings over jeans. I also knew it would be cold in the airports and on the plane so I wore a light, long sweater over my leggings. In addition, I packed a light scarf in my bag because I knew scarves were worn quite a bit by Parisienne women and I could use it as an extra layer around my neck if it was extra chilly. Last, I had a straw fedora hat. I like to wear that hat sometimes with a sundress or at the beach and I didn't want it to get crushed in my bag so I wore it. My friends said I looked "tres francais" in the photo we posted from the airport. I felt "tres francais" as well!

I thanked my husband for driving us, kissed him goodbye, and then we all went into the airport. We checked our luggage, went through security, and sat down to wait. We had a couple of hours until our flight. Marybeth could not believe how small of an airport the Windsor airport was. The same woman that checked our bags helped out in security and also was outside part of the time with flags, directing the planes.

We finally took off! We were so excited! All of the spoken language and signage in the airport and on the plane were both in French and English because we were in Canada and they are bilingual, with each of the languages officially recognized as the nation's languages. It was great to hear the French but it was spoken so fast I couldn't understand it all. I was used to hearing it much slower in all my lessons. I hoped this wasn't setting a precedent for the trip.

Our flight landed in Toronto where we would get a connection to Paris. It was an easy flight and when we got off the plane we walked directly to the International Terminal. There we were able to change our money easily at a currency exchange counter. I wasn't planning on carrying a lot of cash with me on the trip but I knew I needed some cash for the taxi and other things.

We got settled near our gate and prepared for our eight hour layover. We ate lunch, bought some books to read on the airplane, and surfed the internet. Where we were sitting, *each* chair at a table had a tablet for airport guests to use. This kept the girls busy.

While we were waiting, I sat and practiced my French flashcards quite a bit. In the last week leading up to our trip, I suddenly had the idea to write the words and phrases I thought I would use the most in France on flashcards and then study them over and over again until I felt confident using them. I still felt that I couldn't quite recall the words and phrases I wanted to use quick enough and I thought this would give me an added push towards that confidence. I teach my students to use flashcards for quick recall of multiplication math facts, so I knew the benefits of this method. I just wished I had thought of it sooner.

After a long day, our flight was called in the evening and we lined up. Luckily we had chosen our seats earlier and were able to sit all together in the middle section. Here at last was the flight for 'getting to Paris'. I could hardly believe it. We watched movies, read, and slept on the plane. We lost a few hours on the flight with the time change so that essentially we flew "overnight" and arrived at 8:00 a.m. Paris time.

I was nervous as we got off the plane but had to push those nervous feelings aside. I had to get my group together, pick up our luggage in the baggage claim, and find a taxi to take us into Paris. I was used to traveling with my husband or others and relying on them for all the details such as these before but now I knew I had to step up and do it myself. Luckily, Marybeth is very good about helping in situations like that. The girls too, are not timid and very willing to assist and also to look for solutions to confusing things, so we worked well together.

First, we had to figure out where to pick up our luggage. I listened to the announcements, all in French by now, and we followed the signs to the baggage claim. It took quite a while for us to see our luggage on the conveyor belt and we began to think we were not in the right place but eventually our suitcases came out. We managed to tug it all off the belt and were ready to go.

Then the next challenge was getting a taxi. We had to find our way to the taxi area and I also had learned online that we wanted an official taxi with a taxi sign on top of the roof. I had read numerous warnings of unauthorized taxis. The girls and

Marybeth were looking to me to navigate this so I walked up to a gentleman under the 'taxi' sign and spoke to him in French about needing a taxi.

"Excusez-moi, Monsieur. Nous avons besoin un taxi a Paris." He agreed and helped us wheel our suitcases outside. When we got out the door however, he wheeled our luggage over to a regular car, outside of the taxi lane. I looked at Marybeth and both of our eyes got big as we communicated unspokenly about the dangers of this that we had heard about. I told him, no thank you.

"Non, Monsieur. Merci. Nous voulons un taxi normal." He explained that his was an Uber taxi.

"Non, Monsieur. Non, Merci." I said as we took back our suitcases and stepped into the taxi line where the official taxis were lined up outside.

It took a little bit of time before we

found a taxi big enough to fit all of our large suitcases in addition to my carry on. Also, Carissa had brought an extra large suitcase, so that posed a small problem as well. Eventually the taxi clerk waved down a taxi big enough for us and it pulled over. The driver loaded our luggage in the back. The girls and Marybeth jumped in the back seat and I climbed into the front. I handed the driver a 3x5 card with our hotel address on it (a tip I read about online) while I spoke the address out loud, and we were on our way.

Yikes! It was now or never to use my French language skills, I thought. I took a deep breath and jumped right in. I "chatted" with the taxi driver (as Carissa said), all the way to our hotel. I asked how far it was, commented on the weather, and also the traffic. He asked where we were from and I asked him the same. He was from Madagascar, which, I found out from our "chat," was a French speaking province. He told me about an airshow in the area and pointed out the airplanes doing tricks in the sky beyond the highway. It was challenging but I spoke French the whole ride. I was so proud of myself. By the time he dropped us off in the center of Paris, at our hotel, the Hotel de Suede, I had a smile from ear to ear. I was in Paris! I was speaking French! *Getting to Paris* was an exhilarating realization of a lifelong dream!

Chapter 21

Adventures on the Trip: Paris

When we arrived at the Hotel de Suede, it was early afternoon and we were going to meet up with Rebecca and her boyfriend, Chris, for lunch. They had traveled to Barcelona and London in the days before meeting up with us in Paris. Our first days were the last days of their *vacance.* We checked in at the front desk, speaking mostly French and just a little bit of English, and then headed up to our room. It was cute and cozy. It was small and meant only for the two twin beds that were in the center of the back wall. We thought it was funny that the double bed was really just two twins pushed together. To accommodate the four of us though, two cots had been set up as well. We were thankful for that but laughed at how cramped the small room was with the extra beds. We knew we had to make the best of it for our four days in Paris and figured it would be fine. We freshened up, texted Rebecca, and then headed to the lobby to meet them for lunch.

We set out to find our first place to sample French food. There were quaint restaurants all around us near the hotel. The first place that looked good to us was adorable with tables outside, white tablecloths, and walls that opened up to let the fresh air and sunshine into the inner room of the restaurant. We went in, I spoke to the hostess, and then we got seated. We picked up the menus that were on our table and began to look them over. Immediately we realized this restaurant was too fancy and expensive for the simple lunch we were looking for. Meals were full entrees and priced at $28 and $30. I was willing to spend that kind of money on our last night here for a fancy dinner, but not on lunch our first day. We all got up quietly and nonchalantly began to walk out. I spoke to the hostess in French on the way out, explaining what we were looking for "Nous voudrions un déjeuner simple, avec des sandwiches, merci." "We would like a simple lunch, with sandwiches, thank you." It was a bit embarrassing to have made that mistake but not too bad. We remembered that the menus of most of the restaurants were posted outside so we could look them over before we entered next time.

Down the street we came upon another darling place, it seemed to be more like a bar, a brasserie, as they are called in France. These are more informal places with simple

192

food and drinks. We looked over the outside menu and decided it was perfect for our group. The waiter told us he would have a table for six in "juste un peu de temps," so we stepped to the side to wait. As promised, it only took a little bit of time and then we were seated. As soon as the waiter heard us speaking English, he spoke to us in English as well. I spoke to him in French however, intent on using what I had learned.

We ladies ordered wine, because, *pourquoi pas*? The French drank wine with lunch and we were "in it to win it" so we planned that when in France, do as the French do. Chris ordered a beer and we all looked over the menu. Everything sounded delicious! The girls ordered Croque Madame sandwiches, grilled cheese with ham inside and a fried egg on top, *un sandwich francais classique*. Chris ordered a cheeseburger and the rest of us asked for salads. I had planned on waiting until I got to Nice to order a Nicoise salad, since that city is where they originated from, but I ordered one here instead. It was *so* good! So fresh, with greens, tomatoes, hard boiled egg, olives, and surprisingly good anchovies. I don't think I'd ever had anchovies before. To top it off, there was a lovely, light dressing and a beautiful slice of lightly cooked and cooled tuna. I was in heaven the moment I took the first bite. Everyone else enjoyed theirs as well. Our first meal in Paris was a success!

After lunch, we wanted to plan ahead and make sure we didn't have any problems the next day finding the meeting point for our tour of the Eiffel Tower, so we walked to where we would meet our guide the following morning. We used the GPS on our phone to put in the address that we were to meet our tour guide at. At one point while walking, we weren't quite sure in what direction to go. I looked up and saw the Eiffel Tower peeking over the top of some buildings. I couldn't believe it! There it was! It was so real! I pointed to the tower and said to the group "I think we should aim for that direction." They laughed and agreed saying, "Obviously!" We found our meeting point easily, it was only a couple blocks from the Eiffel Tower. We figured since we were so close, we might as well go and take a look at it that day as well. As it came into full view when we rounded a corner, I had a wonderful feeling inside. It really was a beautiful structure. It was magnificent in size and scope and the iron work had so much detail to it. I just could not believe I was standing in front of it. We spent some time admiring it and taking pictures of it and then we walked around exploring some more of the city.

When we saw our first glimpse of the

city, on the taxi ride from the airport, it looked very industrial with lots of tall buildings and a great amount of construction going on with cranes and girders all over the place. My initial thoughts were that it wasn't very attractive and looked similar to other big cities I had been in such as Chicago, Detroit, and New York. As we got closer to the 6th arrondissement where our hotel was located though, the city began to look more like the Paris I had seen and imagined. Small shops, restaurants, and hotels. Shorter buildings with flower boxes outside of windows with open shutters, iconic narrow streets with cafes that spilled out onto the sidewalks. I was relieved and very thankful that Aunt Mary had steered us in that direction when she was helping us choose our hotel.

Then, as we walked around exploring it on foot, I felt deeply happy inside, and so thankful for the opportunity to be there. The architecture was gorgeous, mostly stone buildings with lovely porticos. The detail on the buildings was beautiful and the doors were pieces of artwork in themselves. We walked and walked and then finally stopped for an espresso at a sweet little cafe. I usually order a soy latte at our local Starbucks when I have afternoon coffee but again, when in France... I ordered the typical afternoon espresso that I had learned so many French people partake in daily. The cup the espresso came in was a mini version of a white tea cup. I couldn't get over how small it was. I took the first sip and as I expected, it was very bitter. Since a cube of sugar came with the espresso, on the side, I plunked one half of the cube in my cup in an attempt to make it palatable enough to drink. The sugar did the trick and I was able to enjoy my espresso ~ *a la Parisienne.*

It was *very* hot the week we were in Paris. The temperatures were in the high 90's and broke a record high dating back to 1872. Because of this, the first day and every day that we were there, we rested in the air conditioning in the hotel in the afternoons for a couple of hours, before setting back out to explore the city and find a place for dinner. I'm always cold and usually enjoy being warm in the summer but even for me, the temperatures were tiring. I hated to spend any time at all inside but it was needed in order for us to enjoy our days.

The first night we ventured down to an area called "old town" in St. Germain for dinner. Aunt Mary had told us about this area of Paris that is even more quaint than part of the St. Germain neighborhood that our hotel was in. We used the "Walking Tours of Paris" packet of cards that Aunt Mary had loaned me that had the square drawn in of the area her friend had visited while in Paris. This was the spot that she highly recommended as having great shops and restaurants where the locals rather than tourists frequented. The area was between Rue de Four and Rue Guisarde; and Rue Mabillon and Rue des Canettes. We had no idea which restaurant to choose in this area but ended up at an attractive little place called La Grille Saint Germain. It was right on a corner with an open table right up front outside.

The waiter was friendly and brought over a small table to add to the one already there so that we would have enough seats for us all. Every cafe only had tables for two and so our large group always took up three tables as once. We ended up having a wonderful dinner! I had duck with a delicious red wine sauce. Everyone was very pleased with their dinners too and then as it was getting dark and we were all very tired from jet lag, we decided to get to bed so as to be ready for the next day.

In the morning we woke up and had breakfast at the hotel in the lobby area before going to our tour of the Eiffel Tower. We walked to meet our guide from the Viator.com tour company, and the rest of our group. Our guide was very sweet. She was a student at the Sorbonne University in Paris and spoke very good English. As she walked and we followed, she stopped underneath the tower and explained to us about the tour, how we had passes to skip the line and would be able to go right in, take the elevator up to the main level and have our guided tour there. After that we would be able to go to the summit at the top on our own and stay as long as we liked, admiring the views of Paris.

The tour was amazing! Riding the elevator up was exciting and a bit surprising because it follows a diagonal path, unlike any other elevator I have seen. The views from above were breathtaking. The tour guide gave us a wealth of information. For example, as she pointed out the Louvre to us in the distance, she told us that King Louis the XIV thought that palace was too small for him so he had the Palace of Versailles built instead. Even from so far away, we could see that the Louvre palace was enormous. What kind of man wouldn't think that was big enough, we wondered. This same king, also known as the "Sun King" added real gold to much of the architecture in Paris, to the doors, the fences and more. She told us that whatever gold we see, is *real* gold, not gold paint. Sadly, during World War II, she explained, many of the German soldiers "helped themselves" to the gold while they occupied the city and so to this day, you will not see very much of it. After our tour, she let us go on our way to the summit. The views from there were even more unbelievable than on the main deck. Again and again I just couldn't believe we were there. Finally, our group headed down and walked around the outside of the tower admiring the wrought iron detail on all sides.

We agreed on having lunch picnic style on the lawn beside the tower so we began shopping for our lunch. It was so fun going from shop to shop gathering whatever looked good to us for lunch. We stopped first at a fruit and vegetable market. The fruit looked perfectly ripe. I spoke to the men working there in French and we got raspberries, cherries, tomatoes, cheese and olives. Next we found a *boulangerie* for baguettes, but it was a little more difficult to find a *super marche*. Chris wasn't shy so he asked a gentleman on the street where a supermarket was but the man tried giving directions in French and then asked "Parlez-vous francais?" to Chris and he said no but pointed to me.

"Je parle un peu de francais," I answered "I speak a little," and the gentleman proceeded to give me the directions.

"Tournez a gauche, alors, tournez droite, voila!"

"Merci, Monsieur" I said smiling and we were able to find it in no time. There we purchased some sausage, some foie gras, and of course some wine. We had a magnificent picnic sitting in front of the Eiffel Tower and it was incredible. We ate and talked and looked up at the beauty of the tower, enjoying every bit of it.

Later that night, after another delicious dinner at an outdoor cafe near the tower, we took a cruise on the Seine at twilight to see the view of the city from there. Our tickets were part of a package from the afternoon so again we were able to skip the line. The cruise began and ended at the Eiffel Tower and lasted an hour long. It was a beautiful night! Since the weather was warm, we sat outside on the top deck of the boat as we cruised along admiring all of the ancient buildings and romantic bridges. There were many people enjoying the night along the shore on both sides. They could be seen picnicking, enjoying their wine and friends and generally having a great time. Occasionally a group from shore would call out to our boat and the scores of people on board would answer back. As we returned to the dock, we could see the Eiffel Tower all lit up and then at the stroke of 11:00 p.m., it began a spectacular light show that made the whole tower sparkle and crackle all over. It looked like sparkling Christmas lights twinkling all over it and it lasted for five minutes.

The cruise was a wonderful way to end our second night in Paris.

The next day we got up early to go and visit the Louvre, the iconic and well-known art museum in Paris. We were grateful for the third installment of the ticket package we had purchased that allowed us to skip the line one last time. We went in through the modern glass dome, and were directed down stairs for the main entrance before climbing the escalator and stairs back up to see the main event, which to us was the Mona Lisa painting by Leonardo da Vinci. We had been told by several naysayers that it was very disappointing to look at because it was so small. As we found it and gazed at it ourselves, we didn't feel that way at all. It was a decent size and still very lovely to look at so we were glad that we had seen that first before the crowds made it more difficult to view.

We continued on, seeing more famous pieces in the museum, the Venus de Milo and Eugène Delacroix's *Liberty Leading the People* among others. I enjoyed the paintings by Rembrandt, Vermeer, Botticelli and Caravaggio the most. We wandered through the galleries but it was challenging to take it all in. The girls were bored and after a couple of hours we were ready to go. We had difficulty finding the exit so I asked a guard in French how to find our way out. "Excusez-moi, Monsieur. Ou est la sortie?"

"Vous partez deja?" he asked, "You are leaving already?"

"Oui, Monsieur," I replied, "Les jeunes filles sont pretes." I offered, pointing to the girls. "The young ladies are ready." The guard smiled, knowingly.

We left the museum and walked to Notre Dame. It was our intent to see the inside of the famous church and attend the mass at noon. When we got there however, everyone was hot, tired, and the line outside was very long. We debated for a minute deciding if we would wait in line or not and then our group agreed that we would skip it. I looked longingly back at the church as we walked away but I understood. We found a nice place for lunch and we refreshed ourselves with cold salads, water and *bien sur, du vin.* As we were walking and shopping after lunch, we stumbled upon the Saint Germain des Pres church. I recognized it from my research for the trip. "Can we stop in here?" I asked, and since everyone was feeling much better after lunch and there was *no* line, we all went in. This church is the oldest one in Paris and it was very touching to walk around the inside admiring the details and feeling the history of it. So, no Notre Dame, but yes for the oldest church in the city. It was a fair trade in my opinion.

That night we consulted Yelp, on online review site for our choice of restaurant for dinner. Rebecca uses Yelp all the time in Chicago where she lives, for everything from dentists to coffee shops, etc. This night, Rebecca found a restaurant named Chez Germain at 30 Rue Pierre Leroux. It was a short walk from our hotel. From the moment we walked in, I knew it would be a exceptional dinner. The waiter, who is also the owner, greeted us warmly and sat us down at one of only about five or six tables in the intimate place. The decor was dark red with modern and classic touches. We spoke with the waiter in both English and French and he guided us through the menu choices. After we placed our order for dinner and some bottles of wine, we spoke to him more about his delightful place, where we were from, why we were in Paris and more. When the food came out, not only was it a feast for the eyes, but it was just as much a feast for the palate. Everything was delicious, some of us shared bites from each other's plates in order to share in the pleasure of it all. Altogether, we were there for almost three hours. *C'etait un diner tres incroyable*!

At the hotel, we didn't want the night to end so Chris and Rebecca walked over to a local shop and bought *plus de vin*. The rest of us went to our room to gather what was left of our picnic food from the day before and we all met in the courtyard of the hotel for a nightcap. Our little *fete* went on into the evening and as we talked and laughed the night desk clerk had to come out twice and ask us to quiet down. After the second time we asked him if we could go into the lobby and he agreed "C'est une bonne idee!" So we bought another small bottle of wine from the hotel stock and moved inside. The desk clerk was very sweet to us, he mentioned an unfriendly group of guests that had just left the lobby and he invited us to stay as long as we liked. We talked with him a bit. I could not speak very good French at this point, my memory not being what it was earlier in the night even though my confidence was fine. We talked and laughed until we were out of breath and then we all conceded that it was finally time to say *bonsoir.* What a good night it had been.

The next day was our last day in Paris. We went to brunch at a restaurant outside in the Jardin de Tuileries on the grounds of the Louvre Palace. It was a gorgeous morning and the gardens and fountain were beautiful. After brunch we headed over to the Musee de L'Orangerie, the museum that houses Claude Monet's Water Lilies paintings. I hadn't found any Monet pieces at the Louvre and he is my favorite artist. I had learned before coming to Paris that this museum was quite small, quiet, and never crowded so I thought it would be a perfect antidote to our overwhelming experience at the Louvre the day before. It took a bit of convincing but I assured the group that this museum would be worth visiting.

As anticipated, we purchased our tickets without having to wait in any line and then started toward the door of the first of two oval rooms that house the paintings. When I walked into the first room I was so over-whelmed by the beauty I almost cried. My mouth dropped open as I walked in staring at the breathtaking paintings. The colors were beyond anything I had ever seen in all of my Monet books, note cards, and post-ers. Not only were they stunning paintings, they were immense as well. Each of the four paintings in each room took up a very long wall and stood nearly from floor to ceiling. They were wonderful and everyone else admired them as well. I was so glad we added this unexpected delight to our itinerary for the day.

We headed back to the "old town" area and shopped and just enjoyed walking about seeing as much of the area as we could. The girls bought some clothes, Marybeth found some shoes, and Rebecca purchased an adorable red kerchief type scarf. We even found a Laduree bakery, famous for macarons, the quintessential French cookie. I don't really like sweets but even I had to admit that I wanted to try one of these well-known cookies. We went inside and I spoke to the salesgirl in French, asking how her day was going and a bit about the cookies. We then all chose one and the salesgirl wrapped them up very sweetly for us. Outside we broke open the bag for our taste test and bit into our cookies. They seemed to melt in your mouth. The outer cookie had a wonderful delicate taste with just a hint of crunch, and the inside cream was sweet but not cloyingly so, just enough to awaken your senses without being overwhelming. Just what I want in any sweet, and just what I would expect of a Laduree macaron.

For our last dinner together, we wandered back to "old town," that being our favorite area. Each time we walked to that area it seemed we had gone past some sort of complex that looked like a type of embassy or something. There was no signage on the building but there were flags and armed guards outside. As we walked by that night, the gate was open and when we peered in we could see many lovely people all dressed up, getting out of dark cars and going up the steps into the building. There seemed to be more activity there this last night, an event of some sort. While we walked, we saw more and more armed policeman, on several corners. They were armed with machine guns. It didn't make us nervous, in fact it made us feel more safe.

We chose La Cafe Varenne and sat down outside next to an adorable family, a French mother and her two young daughters. They were finishing up dinner together. It was delightful to hear them speaking back and forth in French, especially the little girls. We ordered and then took in our surroundings, charming streets both to our left and our right and our own handsome young policeman garnishing a machine gun several feet away from us on the corner. We asked the waiter why there were so many policemen out tonight and he told us that just down the *rue* was the residence of the French Prime Minister. Well! Now we knew. We felt very important indeed to be in the same vicinity as the Prime Minister and thought it was very interesting that his residence was in the middle of this district of local shops and restaurants.

Once again, we had a lovely dinner and cherished our last night together. We sauntered slowly back to our hotel, along the sidewalk next to the Prime Minister's residence watching as the armed soldiers walked up and down the street peering into cars that were parked or driving by. We felt very much a part of the local scene by this point. At the hotel, we hugged and kissed and said goodbye to Rebecca and Chris. We would be heading to our next destination the following day and they would be heading home. It had been a remarkable week shared by all. I was grateful for the opportunity to spend my time in Paris with such a great group of friends and family.

Chapter 22

The City of Beaune

Friday morning, we woke up early and took a taxi to the Gare de Bercy train station. It was very interesting at the station because the signage was not very helpful. We knew we didn't have any second chances if we missed our train so we worked together to figure out which track our train was on and make sure that we got on the correct one. We were pretty sure we were headed to the correct train but at that point there were no workers around to ask so as we stood there looking bewildered a very nice French woman who spoke a little English offered to help us. I showed her our tickets and she told me that we had to check the sign at the front of the train to be sure and she began walking toward it. I was fairly certain we had already checked that sign but I followed her to be sure. After we passed several cars and got back to the front, the woman and I checked the sign together and agreed that we were getting on the correct train. I was so thankful for her going out of her way to make sure we were in the right place.

Getting *on* the train was an adventure in itself. We first handed up all of our luggage assembly line style and piled it on the platform in front of the door to the train car. Next we pushed the button to open the door and began loading our luggage on the racks at the front of the car. Marybeth was at the head of the group and as we handed her each piece she placed it on the rack. The doors however kept closing and unlike on American trains where the doors pop back open if they bump an object in their path, these doors just kept closing. It got to be humorous and we were all laughing while trying to keep them open just long enough to pass another piece of luggage through. There was a French family just inside the car next to the rack that was solemnly watching us the whole time. I was trying to laugh quietly and act nonchalant about it all but the others couldn't hold it in. The doors actually closed on Janine's backpack *while* it was on her back essentially pinning her in the door and that was when we all just lost it, laughing uncontrollably. As tears streamed down our faces, I tried to get everyone back under control by whispering under my breath, "Come on you guys, let's get this and get done with it!" It still took several minutes more though because at that point we were doubling over with stomach cramps laughing and trying to hold it in, but eventually we managed to get all of our luggage on the racks and make it to our seats. Taking deep breaths, we all relaxed and prepared for the ride.

As we rode, we listened to the announcements at each stop. The speaker talked very fast and I could only catch glimpses of what he was saying. I could make out that he stated to "gather your personal belongings before you depart" and I could make out the name of the city we stopped in each time - Dijon, Lyon, etc, but that was about it. We knew it would take about four hours to reach the city of Beaune (pronounced 'bone'), so we didn't pay much attention until we got closer. The girls also used their smartphones to track the train and they told us when we were nearly there. We successfully "gathered our personal belongings," our embarrassingly large and multitudinous luggage, and disembarked from the train.

We were going to stay in a Bed and Breakfast this time and it was relatively close to the station in Beaune so we decided to walk there rather than take a taxi. We probably looked pretty silly walking the half mile through the neighborhoods and side streets to the inn, but it seemed even more silly to take a taxi for a six minute ride.

La Villa Fleurie Bed & Breakfast Inn was adorable! It had a stone fence around the front and back yard and a gate at the front entrance. We went in, met the owner and were shown to our rooms on the second floor. Having large suitcases is one thing, carting them up two, rather long flights of stairs at an inn that didn't have an elevator was another thing. We made it up though, laughingly, and to our room, helping each other on the way. Our room was a quaint duplex type room with two twin beds on the main floor, and a stairway up to a loft above with a double bed for the girls to share. Another quaint thing about this room was that the shower and sink were up in the bathroom next to the loft bedroom, and the toilet was in a separate small room on the main bedroom floor.

After unpacking, we spent the day exploring the charming little city of Beaune. We had dinner at a darling cafe and afterwards, listened to a youth orchestra playing in the park at the center of the village. There was a fountain and a carousel there as well. We came to Beaune because we wanted to experience a small village as opposed to the big city of Paris and this night seemed exactly what we were looking for. For our cooking class at The Cook's Atelier the following day we were supposed to meet with the teachers of the class at the Hess Cheese Shop in the center of the town before it began. Wanting to plan ahead again, that night we found the cheese shop easily near the park before we headed back to La Villa Fleurie.

We were so excited the next morning as we readied ourselves for the day. We were anticipating a great day. The cooking class was to begin at 10:00 a.m. and end around 4:00 that afternoon. We walked to the Hess Cheese Shop and began to look around for the teachers. A friendly older woman walked up to us and introduced her daughter and herself. Marjorie Taylor and Kendall Smith Franchini are the mother-daughter duo who own and teach classes out of their atelier in Beaune. Marjorie beckoned to us and some other small groups of women standing nearby to gather around her. She made some quick introductions and then began to explain how our day would go. First, we would go to the farmers market, then we would go to the atelier and cook,

last we would sit down to a wonderful, leisurely seven-course lunch.

Our first stop was the farmers market
that was in the park in front of the cheese
shop. Marjorie and Kendall began by walking with us around the market. They had
been shopping since 8:00 that morning and
explained to us they had already shopped
for the ingredients we would need that afternoon to save time, but they wanted to
show us each stand that they made purchas-
es at and introduce us to the purveyors as
well. We met butchers, fromagers (cheese
makers), farmers, florists, etc. Marjorie told
us a little bit about each one as we went.
"This is Yan, we buy our vegetables from him.
This is Monsieur Vossot , we buy our meat
from him. This is Madame Loichet, (a sweet
grandmother type woman). She always
has the best flowers. We buy our flowers
for the table only from her." It was lovely

to meet every individual and to hear Marjorie expound on the benefits of each one. "As cooks," explained Marjorie, "we feel the most important thing is to source the best quality products and to really develop a relationship with those who produce your food. We are very lucky in Burgundy that we have so many wonderful artisan food producers who are as passionate about their craft, whether they are gardeners, butchers, cheesemakers, etc., as we are about cooking." Her and Kendall believe organic is important "not so much as a sales pitch, but more about the care that goes into the process." They encourage all of their guests to seek out their own trustworthy local producers at their own markets as well. As we walked we admired the luscious food of the market. The colors were phenomenal. The fruits and vegetables looked to be at the peak of freshness. The varieties of everything from olives to lettuces were astounding. This was the most remarkable farmers market I had ever been to. I don't know if it was because it truly was remarkable or if the experience was heightened that much more by being in France.

Next we walked to the atelier down a pleasant little side street where the unassuming cooking school/shop stood tucked between two other shops on either side. We entered through their street level wine and mail order shop and followed Marjorie up a winding wooden staircase to the kitchen on the second level. There we all put on aprons, tucked hand towels into the apron strings, washed our hands and took our places at a long gray, granite work station. Each person had matching cutting boards and other tools needed for the afternoon at their place. The teaching kitchen was beautiful. It had whitewashed walls and dark wood doors, windows, and woodwork. There was a large stove, sink, and numerous copper pans hanging from above. Before we got started we were all brought iced coffee with cream and sugar.

For the next two hours we chopped, stirred, shredded, peeled, sauteed, seared and basically did anything that was asked of us as Marjorie masterfully taught us about the ingredients, methods of prepping them, and demonstrated French culinary techniques for baking, and cooking. Each of us were given a task in turn and the others watched and learned at the same time. We were all just as excited as the next person at each new task. Being in the kitchen had never been so fun. While we were all working hard and following directions from Marjorie, Kendall was interjecting helpful tips and sidenotes as well. She and her assistant were also cleaning up after each portion was prepared, something all of us noted would be especially helpful in our own kitchens back home. They also brought us bottomless glasses of iced water and coffee while we worked.

We prepared gougeres, small cheese puffs; mini cheese souffles; roasted vegetables, including fava beans which I had never cooked or eaten before; rack of veal; butter cake with berries; and madeleine cookies. We learned so much that day and all the while our senses feasted on all of the sights, sounds, tastes, touches, and smells of the atelier.

After preparing the food, we were ushered up another flight of winding stairs to the third floor dining room for our lunch. The modest room was centered with a farmhouse table topped in gray zinc. It was set with white dishes and cloth napkins, antique silverware and clear glass water goblets and wine glasses. The centerpiece was five small glass bottle vases which held one white gerbera daisy in each and tea light candles lit and set into antique silver brioche tins. In the corner was champagne and the delicious gougeres that we had prepared earlier. When we bit into the cheese puffs, it was like a little bite of a cloud, they were so light and they melted in your mouth. We were each given a glass of the bubbly and we toasted to all of our hard work that day.

As we sat down, we introduced ourselves and told a little bit about how we came to attend this wonderful class. I told the story of this being my lifelong dream and how I had planned and saved for a number of years to get there. Marybeth told about being invited to join me, and Carissa and Janine did the same. Besides our group there were two young women in their twenties who were sisters from Canada. One was a nurse and one was in nursing school. Originally it was their parents who were supposed to be in the class but, when their mother couldn't make it at the last minute, their parents encouraged the girls to take their place instead. The young women were adorable and our girls loved talking to them, especially Carissa who was interested in nursing as well. Next to them there were to lovely older ladies from Chicago. One was a school counselor and the other was her friend. In addition there was a freelance photographer who was born in America, grew up in Canada, and who had come to Paris to work and was engaged to a frenchman. With her was her friend, a journalist, Lindsey Tramuta. Lindsey had written an article about The Cook's Atelier for a magazine a while back and she was there that day to attend the class herself, for fun. We learned later from Marjorie that Lindsey was also an author of the book "The New Paris" which had been recently published. Kendall's husband, who ran the wine shop below the studio, drove out to their house in the suburbs while we were eating lunch to pick up their copy of Lindsey's book to show all of us. It was a wonderful group of women and Marjorie commented that it was the first class of all women that they had ever had.

Marjorie and Kendall began pouring wine for us and bringing us the first of our courses. We began with cantaloupe melon slices wrapped in prosciutto. Next came the cheese souffle that we had prepared in mini copper one cup measuring cups. After that we had the roasted vegetables, displayed attractively on white dinner plates, which made the colors stand out against the white background. Fresh, rustic bread and butter came with the roasted vegetables. To lay on top of the vegetables, next came the rack of veal, seared and then roasted after Marybeth had properly "frenched" the bones at the top earlier in the kitchen. Roasted potatoes accompanied the veal. Following the main course we had a cheese and charcuterie course. Expertly displayed on small, wooden cutting boards, the sausages were sliced and fanned out or layered enticingly on the boards along with several cheeses. Finally, came the desserts of which we had not one, but two. First was the butter cake, light and delicious with fresh raspberries that were baked into it after being delicately placed on top before baking by Carissa and Janine. Next were the madeleine cookies, with a faint lemon taste to them. Last, was a white bowl of fresh apricots. They were so appealing, Janine ate *seven* of them.

By the end, we were full, happy, and thoroughly grateful for such a wonderful day. It was nearly 5:30 and we all thought it was about time to leave. As we gathered our things and headed downstairs we decided that we just *had* to have some of the wine we had shared, to take back home with us. Not wanting to travel with wine, we signed up to have it shipped. We left the atelier in a state of utter happiness. "That felt like a little bit of heaven." Janine said, as we all walked down the street back to our hotel. The rest of us couldn't have agreed more.

The balance of our time in Beaune paled in comparison to the day at the cooking class but it was still delightful. The night of the cooking school we bought a bit of cheese, sausage, bread and wine and picnicked outside in the garden of La Villa Fleurie. After we ate and were sitting and reminiscing about our day, the owner of the inn and her visiting daughter came out to sit with us as they ate their dinner. We had a very nice talk, albeit mostly in English, about France,

America, the politics and new presidents of each, and the people of both countries. We talked about the terrorist problems of the world, and the goodness of people to overcome them and get along despite them. It was really nice to share conversation with these ladies.

The following morning we went to mass at the local church in town the Collégiale Notre-Dame de Beaune. I was thrilled since we had missed going to mass at Notre Dame in Paris. This church in the center of Beaune was built in the middle of the twelfth century and the inside displayed intricate frescoes, tapestries, stained glass windows, and side chapels. It was gorgeous! The congregation seemed to be mostly local people as there were two families celebrating baptisms that day. It was lovely to hear the mass said in French and it was easy to follow along since every mass around the world follows the same mass each day.

After mass we visited the local museum, the Hotel Dieu, which was a charitable hospital founded in 1443 by the chancellor for the poor and the most disadvantaged. The outstanding architecture and decoration are a work of art. We borrowed headsets and listened to the story of this amazing place as we walked from room to room. Later we shopped and ate in town before falling off to sleep that night, content with a marvelous stay in Beaune.

Chapter 23

Last Stop, the French Riviera and Nice

Our way to Nice was fraught with a few more challenges than our train trip to Beaune. We started out the morning we were to leave by walking to the train station with all of our luggage. By then I had figured out that if I set my small carry-on suitcase on the top of my large one and rested it against the pull up handle, then I could angle both towards me and roll them together down the street. This helped but it was still a struggle and I was glad when we reached the station.

Once inside, we read the boards and were worried that we didn't see our train and departure time listed. Perplexed, we agreed that I would go to the window and ask the gentleman working there where we were to go for our train. I calmly walked up to the window and asked "Excusez-moi Monsieur. Ou allon-nous pour le train a Nice?" *Where do we go for the train to Nice?*

He answered, "blahblahblahblahblah-blahblah," or at least that is how it sounded to me. Taking a breath I inquired "Plus lentement s'il vous plait?" *Slower please?*

To which he responded "blah - blah - blah - blah -blah." I smiled, nodded my head and

walked back to the others.

"What did he say?" asked Marybeth.

"I have *no* idea" I said as we all laughed together. Okay, so then we knew we had to

try something else. At that point, Carissa realized that we were looking at the screen for "*arrivees*" and we needed the screen for "*departs*" so we all headed to departures side of the station. There we read that we needed to be on the platform across several tracks away, Platform #2 to catch our train. We began walking to the door and just at that time the wheel of my suitcase bumped the edge of a standing sign and I caught it just in time before it hit the floor. Mouth and eyes wide open in surprise, I looked up to see who else had noticed and I saw a bench lined with teenage boys, among others in the station, snickering at us funny Americans. They had already been witnessing our faux pas since we entered the small station, looking at the wrong screen, walking back and forth across the room, not being able to translate the workers words, and now this. I looked at Marybeth and we tried to stifle our laughs as well as my embarrassment but tears ran out of our eyes at the ridiculousness of it all.

We made it to the other train track but we still weren't certain if that was where we needed to be. There were no other signs on that track. I asked a gentleman near us in French if this was the correct spot for the train to Nice and it was "blah, blah, blah" all over again. Did people speak slower in Paris or was it just my imagination? Then we noticed a woman speaking in English to a man and a woman so I walked over to her and asked in English this time, if we were in the correct spot. She looked at my tickets and assured me that yes, we were at the place where our train would arrive in a little while. The couple she was with had the same tickets as us so she said to follow them and we would surely end in Nice. We thanked her and made friends with the English speaking couple and waited with them for the train.

Our biggest challenge was that we had to transfer from the first train to another one in Chalon Sur Saone so we had to make sure we not only got off in the correct city, but that we got back onto the correct train there. We stayed with our new friends, the English speaking couple and when the correct train came to a stop in Chalon Sur Saone we followed them off the train. Again, we were confused as to where we were to get onto the next train. The gentleman inquired and found out that we were to stay right where we were and our train would pick us up there shortly. When it did come, we weren't exactly sure it was our train. Our friends started walking to the end of it and I thought perhaps they were just moving down on the platform. When I asked the man if this was our train and he said yes, and pointed to an electric sign flashing on the side of the train that he thought I had seen and understood. It was flashing the name of the trains *final* stop, Lyon, not *our* stop, Nice.

By the time I could turn around and let Marybeth and the girls know, several minutes had passed and we had to run with our suitcases in order to get to our car and get on in time. We made it but just barely before the train took off. We hoped and prayed we were on the correct train and then sat down for the journey hoping for the best.

Along the way, we took note that no conductors came to check our tickets at all as they had done on the train from Paris to Beaune. Neither on the first train that day or the second one. We were perplexed and wondered if there were any people who ever cheated the system and got on and off without tickets. I guess we'll never know.

We made it to Nice and got off at the Nice train station. I inquired where the taxis were and the gentleman working at the station told me, "Sortir à la porte et ensuite à votre droite." *Go out the door and then to your right.* This I understood clearly. Maybe it was just in the Beaune train station that people spoke quickly to confused Americans.

We got our cab and rode the ten minutes to our hotel, the Residhome Nice Promenade. We checked in and found our room to be the largest one yet. Unknowingly, as we were looking for a hotel to accommodate the four of us, we had made reservations at an apartment style hotel where there was a bedroom with a double bed for the girls, two twin pull out beds in the "living room" area for me and Marybeth, and a kitchenette that included a small refrigerator, microwave, sink and dishwasher. This hotel did not provide clean towels and housekeeping every day like conventional hotels but that was fine with us.

We were excited to unpack and go out right away to see how close we were to the beach since we could not see it from the hotel. The receptionist explained that we were to walk two blocks going around the building across the street and that the beach was right there. It was true. When the beach and the Mediterranean came into view, we could hardly believe our eyes. It was stunning! We shook our heads at the unbelievable beauty of it, the colors, the intensity, and the coastline. We couldn't wait to spend the next day at the beach.

In the morning we walked along the Promenade des Anglais, the stretch of walkway next to the waterfront and found a private beach club for the day. In Nice, the beach is made up of small stones rather than sand and there are alternating areas of public and private beach spots all along the shore. We found a darling blue and white beach club called the Neptune Plage and chose our chairs for the day in the front row next to the sea.

The girls and Marybeth laid in the sun all day while I rented an umbrella opting for shade instead. It is a bit tricky angling an umbrella just so in order for the sun to be blocked. It is more tricky as the day goes on and the sun moves across the sky. As the day progressed, some young French women came and selected the lounge chairs next to us. It was fascinating listening to them talk in their native French tongue. This was the most conversation in French I had heard our whole trip. I tried to eavesdrop nonchalantly as I appeared to be reading my book.

As luck would have it, my umbrella gave off unwanted shade to the young lady next to me since the umbrella was between the both of us. She stood up and lowered the umbrella while I was down at the water taking pictures of the girls. I don't think she realized that I had purchased the umbrella for my shade for the day. As I walked back to my chair, I tried to form the words in my mind of how to explain it to her in French, so that I wouldn't look like an obnoxious American who did not speak their language. "Excusez-moi Mademoiselle," I began. "C'est pour moi." *That's for me,* I explained. "Je vais utiliser cette parapluie au lieu." *I am going to use this umbrella instead,* as I pointed to the umbrella on the other side of me.

"Oh!" she replied looking surprised.

"C'est bien?" I asked her as I opened the other umbrella, *That's good?* I pointed to the shade now covering only my chair and not hers.

"Oui, merci" she answered, and smiled. I smiled back and it was all settled. I think she appreciated my efforts and I appreciated being able to explain myself in French as well.

One thing that was noticeably different

about this beach than our American beaches other than the stones vs. the sand, was the topless women sunbathing. We had been cautioned about this back in the States when we mentioned to our friends and families that we were going to the beach in France. We didn't think it would bother us, and it didn't. There weren't really very many women who were topless and it was always a grandma aged woman who sat there enjoying the sun that way. Never once did we see anyone younger than that. One thing that did bother us was the number of women with unshaved armpits. Lovely women with darling swimsuits and figures would surprise us time and again when they raised their arms to show a tuft of hair where we were accustomed to to seeing a smooth, shaved area. That is one part of the French culture that I would not be adopting.

All day our girls alternated between

laying in the sun and swimming in the surf. We spent the day mesmerized by the blues of the Mediterranean contrasted by the white of the rolling waves. At lunch, we walked in to the cafe and ordered a lovely lunch that we enjoyed as we gazed out at the sea. We never got tired of looking at it.

After a full day in the sun, we were ready to get cleaned up and go to dinner. We walked down the Promenade, much farther this time, down to an area called "old town" about a half an hour's walk away. It was an attractive area with very interesting architecture and a town square surrounded by many restaurants. We stopped in one and had a wonderful meal starting with a cheese and charcuterie board of local cheeses and meats. After dinner we walked back enjoying the sunset over the horizon. There were local music artists playing along the board-walk and vendors selling their wares as couples, families and others walked by. It was a lovely night.

The next day it was supposed to rain so we decided to go shopping instead of to the beach. We walked back to "old town" and visited all the little shops looking for souvenirs and gifts to bring home. The shops were tiny and the streets between them were very narrow. It was an adorable area. We also realized that there were more authentic looking restaurants the deeper you went into "old town." Along our way, we bought some food for lunch and decided that we would picnic on the rooftop of our hotel. It was a covered area with open walls to view the Cote d'Azur, the French Riviera. We purchased a baguette, some cheese, and some sausage. Back at the hotel as the storm swept in for the afternoon we enjoyed our lunch as we watched it roll in. We finished just as it began to rain hard and we went inside for a nap before dinner.

The rain stopped and the sun came out to welcome us on our walk down the Promenade once more for dinner. This time we chose a quaint little restaurant tucked far back in to the old town area and enjoyed a nice, leisurely meal out of the touristy section that we were first acquainted with. After dinner, the girls and Marybeth enjoyed some delicious artisanal ice cream cones on the way back to our hotel.

The following day we headed to the beach again and the Neptune Plage. This day; however, was different from the last in that the wind was fierce as it whipped through the beach club so intensely that we weren't able to put up any umbrellas for shade. The swimming area was closed because the waves were dangerous to swim in and indeed you only saw locals out in the public beach area venturing into the water that day. The lifeguard in our beach club was standing up and on guard all day watching for any help that was needed. The waves became so big over the course of the afternoon that we had to move back not one but two rows so that the beach chairs could be stacked and put away since the waves were coming up so far on to the beach. It still was a beautiful day though and the breeze kept us from feeling the sweltering heat.

That night we went out for our last dinner in France. It was sad but also special. We asked our receptionist at the Residhome for a recommendation for dinner and she told us about a place called Le Melody, just a few blocks down the street.We were not too disappointed to not have to walk all the way back to old town for a nice dinner. Le Melody was a charming little place. As we stood on the sidewalk reading the menu posted outside, I was concerned because there didn't seem to be anything on it for Carissa. Of our group, she was the choosiest when it came to eating. For the past few days she had eaten a couple cheese pizzas, and even a Nicoise cheeseburger in an attempt to find something she liked. The hostess asked us if we wanted to come inside the open door to Le Melody. I said I wasn't sure. "Il n' y a rien pour la jeune fille." *There is nothing for the young lady.* I explained as I pointed to the menu.

"Elle voudrait des 'chicken nuggets'?" she asked and we all laughed. Yes, she would like some chicken nuggets. Carissa lived on chicken nuggets at home. "Je vais demander le chef." *I will ask the chef,* she offered and when I nodded, she tucked inside and came back announcing that not only would the chef create some chicken nuggets for Carissa, that he would make her some *"pomme frites"*, *French fries* as well. We all agreed and went inside.

Inside it was decorated with white walls and white leather booths. There were white tablecloths and touches of black and dark pink around the room, including fresh pink flowers on the table. The table was set elegantly and we ordered a wonderful three course meal beginning with an amuse bouche of mushroom mousse, then our entrees and dessert. For dessert, we were given a sampling plate of sorbet, chocolate lava cake, creme caramel, cheesecake and an espresso. Everything was delicious. We walked back pleased with our choice of place and our last dinner in France, we were to leave for home the next morning.

Chapter 24

———

Reflections After the Trip

Reflecting back on my trip, I asked myself "What did I take away from it? What did I notice, observe, and learn? What changes might have occurred within me because of it? Here are some of the thoughts, ideas, and beliefs I realized after I came home:

• *People in Paris are very friendly.* We had been warned before this trip by many people giving us advice that Parisians are very rude. We didn't experience that at all. The Parisian men and women were friendly wherever we went, in museums, at shops, even on the street. These were not just those in the tourist profession either, those selling us something, it was even people we met on the street or around the area. We were also told that if you didn't speak English, then the Parisian people were even more rude to tourists. Again, we didn't experience that at all. No one else in our group spoke French except me and when they spoke to the French in English, usually they were met with a smile and English speaking back. If the French person didn't speak much English, they still gave a smile and asked *"Parlez-vous francais?"*, which is when I would step in and answer *"Oui!"*

• *The baguettes in Paris really are as good as everyone says they are.* We tried them in the other cities that we went to and never experienced the same taste and texture as lovely as those baguettes in Paris. I'm on a mission now that I am home to visit some local bakeries and try out their baguette recipes. Now I have the real thing to compare them too.

• *I found it to be very true that Parisienne women dress quite nicely* when out and about shopping and running errands. Each woman we passed in Paris, no matter the age from young to middle to elderly, was nicely arrayed in a becoming dress with sandals or walking shoes. It was a stark contrast to the ultra casual, athleisure wear or even frumpy looks worn by so many American women when running errands. We commented to each other as we walked the streets of Paris on the ladies dresses again and again in our group (Chris excluded of course). It was very nice to see.

• *I want more "beautiful" things in my life.* Paris truly was a beautiful city. From the architecture, to the food both in stores and restaurants, to the art, to the streets, parks, street style, cafes and more, everywhere you looked was beauty. It really struck me all this beauty and it had a calming and peaceful affect on me. Even the little things in Paris and France itself were beautiful. I also noticed a distinct absence of any and all things plastic. I began noticing it first at our hotel, then the restaurants, the stores, the Cook's Atelier in Beaune, and in Nice. There were no plastic soap dispensers in the bathrooms; no plastic bins, containers, or bags in the shops; no plastic in the cafes and restaurants, nothing. Everything was made out of wood, metal, glass, or natural fibers. Everything was lovely and not gaudy. It was strikingly different from what I am used to seeing in my city and also in my home.

When I came home, I decided to make a change in my own life because of this noticeable difference. No longer would I buy the plastic hand soap dispensers for my bathrooms, even if they were the cute seasonal ones. No more would I buy unseemly colorful plastic bins to contain things around the house or in my classroom. Nevermore would I accept plastic bag after plastic bag from every shop, store, or market. I would look to the French influence and begin to find things made of natural materials to take the place of even the mundane things in my life.

I purchased a clear glass liter sized water bottle to hold our drinking water both in the refrigerator and more importantly on our dinner table. I purchased metal hand soap dispensers for the bathrooms and I began to slowly replace every garish bin I had with those made from wood or fiber.

• *People are as much the same as they are different.* For all the differences in our cultures, I find that in person, people are much the same. The people we met at the hotels, restaurants, and shops aren't all that different from us. They may speak a different language and perhaps focus on different things than we as Americans do, but they love their country, their families, and their way of life, just the same as us. The taxi drivers in France are the same hardworking people that we have here. The mother eating dinner out with her children guides them in table manners and conversation just as we mothers do. The shopkeepers have willing smiles and are helpful to pleasant customers just as we have in our stores.

• *I've read Lindsey's book "The New Paris" and really enjoyed it.* It was a great read; fun and interesting at the same time. Lindsey introduces the reader to some changes in Paris that are occurring these days, changes in eating out, coffee, drinks, sweets, products, and places in the city.

In the book, Lindsey presents herself as a sort of self-described "amateur" of sorts when it comes to some of the new trends that she describes. When she outlines the new craft beer movement, she admits that she, along with most French people, used to think of beer simply as a cheap party drink and not the fine tasting brews that are being created today. When she expresses being surprised by the horrible taste of the classic Parisian espresso, she is describing what most tourists thought of their first taste, and our hope in the modern baristas bringing delicious tasting coffee to Paris at last.

If you have experience with any of the topics she presents, you recognize the nuances that Lindsey mentions about each one. If you are new to the topics, you feel as though you have the ability to learn and experience them just as Lindsey did. You feel as though they are within reach and not at all unattainable. Her writing is very personable. It makes you feel like a friend is explaining these new trends to you, not an academic high-brow who is just reporting the latest news. I loved the parts that she added about her personal life, about moving to Paris, her thoughts and observations, and times with her husband.

- *I am confident that I can do what I set myself out to do with hard work and perseverance.* Planning the trip, saving for it, and learning the language was not easy, but then most good things in life aren't easy. I always believed that I could do anything if I made the right plan and took all of the necessary steps to make it happen, this trip just solidified my theory on that.

- *That even though the French culture has a lot to offer, so does our American way of life.* I still concede that I like some French ways better than American ways. Things like dressing simply, eating long leisurely meals, and raising children, but I also like some American things better, like smiling a lot, even at strangers when you walk down the street; believing you can do and change things if you work hard; and multi-tasking.

- I love my life here in America.
- It truly was a trip of a lifetime!

About the author

Stephanie Gidley is a fourth grade teacher, wife and mother of three. She was a stay-at-home mom for a number of years and lately returned to school to finish her degree and embark on a teaching career. She lives in Livonia, Michigan, a typical middle-class, suburban neighborhood. By balancing work, family, and a tight teacher budget, she managed to plan and save for a long dreamed of trip to Paris and wrote about it to inspire others to accomplish similar goals. Visit the author's website at http://penciledin.com/stephaniegidley to view photos from her trip to France.

Made in the USA
Columbia, SC
24 July 2018